A MESSAGE FROM CHICKEN HOUSE

I live in the countryside but, even so, I don't pay enough attention to nature. *By Ash, Oak and Thorn* is a truly beautiful tale of what happens when we start really *seeing* the wonderful and endangered world we live in. Melissa Harrison's reimagining of B.B.'s classic stories of yesteryear couldn't be timelier. She follows three little people – miniature guardians and protectors of nature – who are themselves literally disappearing, and who have to journey to find out why. With only bravery, resourcefulness and a few animal friends to guide them, they begin to discover what can be done. Perhaps, when you've read this, you'll be inspired to help too!

BARRY CUNNINGHAM
Publisher
Chicken House

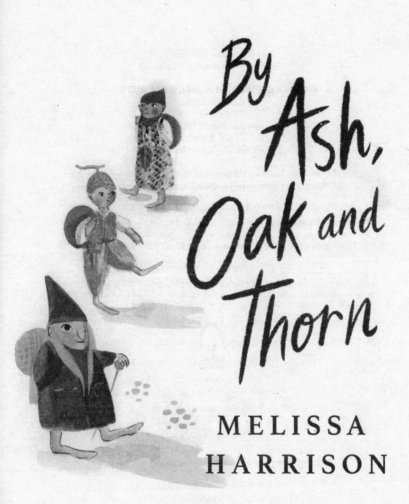

By Ash, Oak and Thorn

MELISSA HARRISON

Chicken House

2 Palmer Street, Frome, Somerset BA11 1DS
www.chickenhousebooks.com

Text © Melissa Harrison 2021
Illustration © Lauren O'Hara 2021

First published in Great Britain in 2021
Chicken House
2 Palmer Street
Frome, Somerset BA11 1DS
United Kingdom
www.chickenhousebooks.com

Cover and interior design by Helen Crawford-White
Typeset by Dorchester Typesetting Group Ltd
Printed and bound in Great Britain by CPI Group (UK) Ltd, Croydon CR0 4YY

FSC
www.fsc.org
MIX
Paper from
responsible sources
FSC® C020471

1 3 5 7 9 10 8 6 4 2

British Library Cataloguing in Publication data available.

PB ISBN 978-1-913322-12-0
eISBN 978-1-913322-94-6

We peer between the intricate stems
of the grass forests and see the
ground-floor people about their
business of living: grasshoppers, ants,
beetles and a host of tiny creatures
that hurry this way and that . . .

B.B., from the preface to
*The Wild Lone: The Story
of a Pytchley Fox*

Contents

Part III Thorn

ASH

1

A spring morning

*In which we meet Moss, Burnet
and Cumulus, and a peculiar
thing is discovered.*

It was the kind of March day that feels springish,
despite the weather not yet having warmed up:
yellow crocuses bloomed on the verges, the leafless
hedges were sprinkled with buds like tiny green
fairy lights about to be switched on, and the sky was
very blue. That kind of day only comes at the very
tail end of winter, and it makes everything feel
fizzy and exciting. It was just the sort of day for
something unusual to occur.

In the garden of 52 Ash Row, next to the trampoline, was an ancient tree with an interesting-
looking hole at the bottom of its trunk. Soon it
would put out fresh new leaves and some frilly,
green-and-burgundy flowers, and then become a
tall green castle with a thousand things living
secretly in it – and soon after that, summer would

come. But for now, the old tree was leafless, and would remain so for many days to come.

The lawn around it was smooth and green, without any daisies or dandelions, and near the house the earth had been covered up with wooden decking. But through the neat and narrow flower beds around the edges of the garden wound secret paths made by wild creatures – some of them known to humans, and some not at all.

A blackbird flew in from next door's garden and landed on one of the lower twigs of the ash, which bobbed under his weight. Then he opened his yellow beak and sang for the very first time since the summer holidays last year, warbling loudly to anyone who cared to listen: *Yes, hello, would you believe it, can I just have your attention please, thank you all for listening, I just wanted to mention . . . that it's SPRING!*

At that exact moment, something appeared in the interesting-looking hole in the old tree's trunk. If Maya and Ben, who lived at number 52, had happened to be nearby, they would have thought it was just some bird or other; but they were at school and knew nothing about it – and anyway they weren't really the noticing (or the listening) types. They hadn't yet discovered that the first blackbird song of spring is the signal for an ancient race of tiny people known as the Hidden Folk to wake from their winter sleep, or that for more than two whole centuries – long before the house or its garden even existed – the ash tree in their garden had had three of these secretive creatures living in its gnarled and hollow trunk.

Out into the sunshine stepped a figure about as tall as your hand is long, with nut-brown skin. Moss (for that was the person's name) was wearing an outfit made of waterproof onion skin, the trousers held up by a red string belt, a cap made from an acorn cup with the twig still jauntily attached, and no shoes.

'Hello, Mr B,' said Moss, squinting up to where the blackbird still warbled. 'Did you have a good winter?'

'Oh, there you are!' said the blackbird, hopping down from his twig to the lawn. 'Hello, Moss. Not bad, thanks for asking, though one could always do with a few more worms, don't you find? Are you all well in there? Did you have a good sleep?'

'Yes, we're all well, thank you. I expect the others will be up and about before long. How's Mrs B, is she all right?'

Just then another little figure stepped out of the hole in the tree, yawning and rubbing its eyes.

Burnet, who was a little bit broader than Moss and a few centuries older, wore a sort of kilt and a fancy waistcoat made from the shed skin of an adder, and carried a much-sharpened metal blade on which the legend STANLEY could still be read – though who Stanley was is anyone's guess. A restless, outdoors kind of person, Burnet was the type who always likes to be up and doing, and finds it terribly hard to be quiet or sit still.

'Morning, all. Well, well, well, another spring! Do you know, I could really do with a proper adventure. I get incredibly bored sometimes, don't you? We haven't even been out of this garden in, ooh, nearly a hundred cuckoo summers!' (A 'cuckoo summer' is the Hidden Folk's term for a year – though, come to think of it, none of them had heard a cuckoo in summer for quite a long time.)

'Blimey!' said the blackbird, whose first name was Bob (though nobody used it). 'A hundred cuckoo summers is a long time to stay in one place. D'you mean you haven't ever been next door, where all the bird feeders are? You really should. And you've never seen the place where all the children spend the day? It's amazing – at lunchtime they drop all sorts of interesting things to eat, like rice cakes, and raisins, bits of apple . . .'

'And chips!' came a warble from a nearby twig, where a starling had just landed with an unnecessary flourish. 'All right, everyone?'

'Hi, Spangle!' laughed Moss and Burnet together. They were both so pleased the cheeky little bird had made it safely back from the starlings' winter conference on the east coast.

'Mmmm, *chips . . .*' said Bob dreamily.

'You all right there, Mr B?' said Spangle. Compared to the soberly feathered blackbird, the cheeky starling was resplendent in his spring plumage, which shimmered as iridescent as petrol in a puddle and was covered in little white arrows.

'Oh, sorry. Hello, Spangle,' said Bob. 'Don't you look smart?'

'That is correct. Now, what's occurring?' asked the starling, settling his feathers and fixing them all with a beady eye.

'Mr B was just saying we should get out more,' explained Moss. 'But we don't have wings like you two – it's not so easy for us to go exploring. Especially if we want to be home in time for bed, which I do.'

'He's not wrong, though – there's a lot to see round these ends,' said Spangle. 'I know you're all, like, *settled* and *safe* in Ash Row, but there's a big

7

Wild World out there, you get me? Not to mention next door.'

'Is Cumulus awake yet?' asked Moss, to change the subject, for all the talk of exploring and adventuring was making Burnet look extremely restless. 'It's such a beautiful spring day, I'd hate anyone to miss out.'

And then there were three little figures gathered at the base of the old ash in the corner of the garden – which is an extraordinary thing when you think about it, though most humans don't. There they were, as plain as day: Moss, the youngest, in onion-skin outfit and acorn-cup hat; broad Burnet in kilt and snakeskin waistcoat, carrying a trusty 'Stanley' knife; and now the oldest (and wisest) of the trio, Cumulus, who had only one eye and long white hair, and wore a crumpled green robe and matching hat. None wore shoes, for the soles of their feet were tough and usefully calloused; their legs and arms were hairy, for warmth.

'At last! Hello, Cumulus!' cried Burnet, offering their ancient friend a hug.

'Happy spring!' said Moss, smiling. But Cumulus's face looked serious, rather than cheerful.

'Good morning, everyone. I'm sorry to say that something rather worrying has happened . . .'

But just then, Bob took off, clucking and shouting hysterically in that alarming way blackbirds have, skimming over the garden fence and making for next-door's tangled shrubs.

'By the great god Pan! What's got into *him*?' exclaimed Moss – but then they heard it too: the back door swinging open, and someone coming out. Spangle followed the blackbird over the fence, while the three little figures whisked themselves into the hole in the ash tree's trunk.

Inside, everything was perfectly shipshape. The floor was of beaten earth, regularly swept clean by Moss with a soft broom made from a wood-pigeon's tail feather (Moss was very house-proud, unlike Burnet). In the centre was a beautiful round mat newly woven each autumn from long strands of dry grass. The lofty chamber extended up into the ash trunk, which had become quite hollow over the years; although that's perfectly normal in old trees, this one was also ill with a new disease caused by a fungus – though nobody knew that yet.

Lower down, the walls had been cleverly fitted with all sorts of tiny cupboards and cabinets in which the trio kept their belongings, including their three sleeping bags woven from spider silk and stuffed with the soft white fluff that blows off poplar trees each spring. At the very back of the room was a stack of snail shells, each with a neat wooden bung and label showing the date. They contained an excellent cordial made from windfall fruit and wild flowers, only to be enjoyed on very special occasions.

'You were saying . . . ?' said Moss to Cumulus.

'Yes. So the thing is – I don't want to worry either of you, and it doesn't hurt or anything, but . . .'

Cumulus held up one hand – and Moss and Burnet gasped, for the shaft of sunlight from the open door shone straight through it. The green sleeve of Cumulus's robe was there, and the wrist, but the palm had become slightly transparent, and the fingertips could barely be seen at all.

'Pan protect us,' whispered Burnet.

'Odd, isn't it?' said Cumulus. 'I noticed it as soon as I woke up. My hand is still there. I can still hold things, and – I don't know – secretly pick my nose or whatever. I just seem to be, well . . . fading away.'

2

A plan is hatched

*Not everyone fancies an
adventure – but the weather
has other ideas.*

Moss, Cumulus and Burnet sat cross-legged in the safety of the hollow ash tree, staring at Cumulus's strangely transparent hand.

'Have you ever heard of anything like this happening before?' asked Moss.

'Not in all the Wild World,' said Cumulus. 'Not to Hidden Folk, or animals, or Mortalkind, or *anyone.*'

'And it doesn't hurt?' asked Burnet.

'Not a bit.'

'Well, that's something.'

'Yes . . . only – what if it doesn't stop? What if more of me disappears?'

'And what if it happens to the rest of us, too?' quavered Moss.

At this, they quickly checked all the parts of

11

their bodies: their hands and feet, legs, arms and elbows. They peered down inside their clothes at their tummies, and carefully counted two knees each under their respective trousers, kilts and robes.

'All of me is present and correct,' said Burnet. 'Everyone else? Good.'

'This means something big, I can feel it,' said Cumulus. 'Something is starting to change, but I don't know what. I've had this feeling before, though, hundreds of cuckoo summers ago.'

'Oh, don't say that!' said Moss, with a shiver. 'I just want everything to stay the same, for ever and always.'

'You know that's impossible,' said Burnet. 'You might be the youngest, but you've been in the Wild World for long enough to know that everything changes all the time.'

'Yes, but . . . I don't like very sudden changes, or when things get worse,' said Moss. 'I only like change when it's good.'

'But you can't always tell how it's going to turn out, can you?' asked Burnet. 'You have to wait and see. Take the last Ice Age: bit worrying at first, then *really* boring and quite chilly, but it turned out all right in the end.'

'How much do you remember from back then,

Burnet?' asked Cumulus. 'You know, the Old Time, before Mortals; when Pan first put us in charge of the Wild World.'

'Not a great deal,' replied Burnet. 'A few images and impressions. It feels like trying to remember a dream.'

Cumulus nodded. 'Moss won't recall much of that world, of course, being the youngest. But I do. I remember it well.'

'Do you remember dinosaurs?' asked Moss, eyes wide.

'I do! Marvellous creatures, some of them. And so funny! Honestly, you'll never meet a better comedian than a brachiosaurus. Some were a bit *much*, of course – gigantoraptors were just plain weird, and I never met a triceratops you could trust. I miss good old archaeopteryx, and the lovely woolly mammoths that came later; and wisents, and burbots, and auks – you know, the really big ones – oh! and those extraordinary blue butterflies you never see nowadays. I miss everything that's passed out of the Wild World, even the tiny things.'

'And what was it like when Mortals first came?' asked Moss.

'Well, there wasn't much change at first – or if there was, I didn't notice. They spoke the Wild

Argot, lived as wild creatures do, and only slowly multiplied – which didn't really concern us. There are loads and *loads* of beetles, for instance, and nobody minds. Even when Mortals learnt how to farm, our kind didn't much worry about them; in fact, we quite enjoyed all the new places they made for us to look after, like the woods they planted for timber, and the hedges, and millponds.'

'I do love a nice, thick hedge,' said Moss.

'Oh, me too,' agreed Burnet. 'Doesn't everyone?'

'But now I can see that when they began to control the Wild World it was the end of our time as guardians. With Mortals taking charge and making big changes, it got harder and harder for us to look after all the trees and plants and wild creatures that lived on our patch. And now, of course, we live just like the animals – which is a fine life, of course. But I do miss having a *job*, you know?'

'Me too,' said Burnet. 'My patch was a beautiful wood of lime trees, lived in by generations of wild boar; I kept it safe, come what may, and made sure it was a good home for all the wild creatures who needed it. You should have seen the stripy little piglets every springtime, and the way the spring leaves danced in the breeze!'

'What became of it?' asked Cumulus. They all

knew what had happened, of course, but sometimes it's important to let your friends tell their stories more than once.

'It was cut down to make furniture,' said Burnet, eyes shining with tears. 'And then I – I had to move away.'

The others nodded in sympathy. They too had stories to tell of the special places they had once looked after: Moss's wildflower meadow, and Cumulus's peaceful pond.

'And . . . Mortals are the guardians of the Wild World now?' asked Moss.

Cumulus frowned. 'That must be how Pan has decreed it . . . though they might not have realized it yet.'

Cumulus felt a bit self-conscious about having an invisible hand, so for the first time Moss and Burnet went to greet the Garden People without their friend. They introduced themselves to new arrivals, like the troupe of cheerful parakeets who'd taken to swinging by, they caught up with the sparrow gang who roosted next door, and chatted to Whiskers the mouse – nearly two hundred generations of his family had lived their short lives under number 52.

Wherever they went, they asked for all the winter gossip, for each year Moss liked to compose a ballad. A ballad is a song that tells a story, but if you don't want to sing it (and Moss's singing voice was really terrible) you can recite it like a poem instead. The ballad was a good way to remember everything that had happened at Ash Row since the last cuckoo summer. For the most part, the other creatures enjoyed it – except when it showed them up for doing something naughty, like when Creep the dunnock secretly had three boyfriends, or one of the local squirrels ate all the great tits' eggs.

'Of course, it's just for fun,' Moss told Carlos the parakeet. 'I know I could never be a *proper* balladeer, like in the Old Time.' For the great legends and sagas of their kind went back thousands of years and were extremely sacred. It didn't seem possible that Moss's made-up story-songs could be the same thing.

At about teatime a brisk wind got up and the sky clouded over.

'Ooh, I don't like the look of that,' said Burnet, shinning to the top of a daffodil to get a better view of the darkening horizon to the west. Despite acting the fool at times, Burnet was by far the best of the three at telling the weather, and had an excellent sense of direction, too. 'Let's go home and check on Cumulus – that hand may not be painful or anything, but I'm still a bit worried about our dear old friend.'

The daffodil's yellow trumpet dipped slowly, depositing the little figure gently back into the flower bed.

'A spot of rain is just the thing at this time of the year,' said Moss. 'It gets everything growing, doesn't it? And we could certainly do with a few more weeds and wild flowers in this garden – the Mortals keep pulling them up, Pan only knows why, and the flowers they plant aren't the kind the bees like.'

Still, it would be a relief to get back to the ash; Moss was the kind of creature who needs some quiet time after lots of socializing. Burnet, on the other hand, could play with friends for hours.

'There's worse than a bit of rain coming,' replied Burnet. 'I think we might be in for a storm!'

They trooped back to the hollow tree, and although one of the grown-ups who lived in the house happened to be looking out of the window just at that moment, wondering if it would be wise to fetch the washing in from where it flapped and billowed on the line, they didn't notice a thing.

Inside they found Cumulus sitting quietly on the floor, looking through a small pile of sand. The grains had been collected over several centuries, and from many places. Some were beautiful colours, or had rare, complicated patterns; others were tiny fragments of coral, or microscopic fossils.

'Sorting through your collection?' asked Moss.

'I just like to look at them sometimes. They remind me of ages gone by,' said Cumulus, putting the sand grains carefully back into their little wooden box, one by one. 'How are the Garden People getting on? Everyone well?'

'All well,' replied Moss. 'The mice have had lots of babies again, and there's a brimstone butterfly fresh out of hibernation – goes by the name of Joan. We couldn't find Furzepig the hedgehog anywhere, though.'

Burnet fetched some dried lichen and a few twigs which were stacked neatly by the entrance and lit a fire using chips of flint which, struck together in the right way, made a spark. Safely lighting a fire was something they had done so many times over the centuries that it had a kind of grace to it: each could do it quickly and perfectly, and almost without thinking. It's often like that when a creature of any kind (even Mortals!) have practised a tricky thing over and over, and it is always a joy to watch.

Moss, who was the best of the three at cooking, took conker bread, honey cake, some dried blackberries and three smoked grasshoppers from the cupboards (these taste a bit like smoky-bacon crisps, but more chewy). Eating the 'spare' crumbs of honey cake was irresistible, for Moss liked food so much it was sometimes hard to share things out fairly – especially if there was nobody to see.

'Pan's teeth, it's getting windy,' said Burnet, as the huge branches of the ash far above them began to sway and creak. 'Of course, this time of year is often a bit blustery. It's only to be expected.'

'That's true,' said Moss. 'And anyway, we're quite safe here. Aren't we, Cumulus?'

There was a long pause while their old friend chewed a particularly stringy bit of grasshopper leg, holding it in a transparent hand, which made it look as if it were floating. At last Cumulus swallowed, then broke off another piece of honey cake and continued to gaze into the fire.

'Are you all right? You've been awfully quiet

today,' said Burnet. 'You must be really worried about your hand.'

'Yes, I am a bit. And – well, I've been thinking about our country cousins. You remember Dodder, Baldmoney, Cloudberry, and dear Sneezewort?'

'We haven't heard from them in a hundred cuckoo summers!' said Moss. 'Do they still live beside that stream in the countryside – the Folly Brook, wasn't it?'

'That's it,' said Cumulus. 'Dodder is one of the last of our kind still to look after the same place since the Old Time: a bend in a stream, where generations of oak trees have always grown.'

'That sounds like heaven,' said Moss, dreamily.

'I wish they lived a little closer,' said Cumulus. 'I was thinking they might be able to tell us something about this . . . well, this disappearing. Sneezewort knew a thing or two about herbs and medicines, and Dodder's even more ancient than me, did you know that? Dodder might know what to do.'

'You know who else might? Robin Goodfellow.'

'That's true, Moss, being the very first of the Hidden Folk, and the oldest and wisest. We did meet once, back in the time of the Romans, but I'm afraid I've no idea where in the Wild World Robin lives now.'

'I know!' Burnet said suddenly. 'Why don't we go on an expedition – to visit the Folly Brook! I can navigate to begin with, and once we're out in the countryside proper we can ask the birds to help us. Mr B's right, and Spangle, too: we've been stuck here in Ash Row for far too long.'

The three of them sat around the fire as the garden grew dark, the branches above them groaned ominously in the wind and fat drops of rain began to fall. They talked and talked as the lights in the houses went out, one by one. Sometimes it seemed as though they were all set on staying put where it was safe, and then Cumulus would point out that there really was no other way to find out what the fading meant, and the conversation would shift until it seemed as though they definitely, *definitely* would go and visit their cousins by the Folly Brook.

But Moss really didn't want to leave their dear, familiar home in the ash tree, or the beloved garden where all their friends lived. They all missed the places they had once looked after, of course; but those distant memories weren't so strong for Moss. What counted was Ash Row, even though it wasn't a row of trees beside a field any more, but a rather ordinary garden surrounded by streets of Mortals' houses – streets they'd never explored. The truth was, Moss couldn't really picture the world beyond the high fences of the garden, and when you can't imagine something, it can feel far more scary than it really is.

At last they grew too tired to continue arguing, so they fetched their sleeping bags, curled up warm and snug, and fell asleep.

It was a stormy night, with sudden gusts that snatched up crisp packets and plastic plant pots and made them dance down Ash Row. Most of the local cats stayed indoors, though the foxes braved the weather and trotted around all night on their foxy business. Thunder muttered and lightning flickered and flashed, at first distantly and then much closer, first striking a distant tower block, and then the spire of a nearby church as thunder rent the air directly overhead.

Several times during the night Moss muttered and thrashed about, and once let out a cry. Burnet carried on snoring, but Cumulus, who was lying awake and enjoying the exciting electrical energy in the atmosphere, came and sat by Moss's sleeping bag in the darkness and murmured a quiet rhyme of reassurance until the bad dream had passed. It was a very ancient poem, and while nobody really knew what it meant any more, it had in fact been given to the Hidden Folk by the oldest of their kind, Robin Goodfellow, back in the Old Time:

> *Ash, oak and thorn*
> *Were at the world's dawn.*
> *Rowan and yew*
> *Will make it anew . . .*

As the night wore on the rain gradually lessened and the thunderstorm ran out of energy and faded away. By the time the first bird sang at dawn, the sky over Ash Row was rinsed fresh and clear, ready for a new day.

It was then that the old, rotten tree gave a great shiver, uttered an eerie, creaking groan – and ripped entirely in two. Each half fell outwards and down with a thunderous crash, smashing one of the garden fences and covering the lawn and the flower beds, the trampoline and shed with a wreckage of broken branches and billions of twigs, so that the garden was completely unrecognizable. Inside the Mortals' house, the grown-ups and children were woken from sleep and sat up in their beds with thumping hearts and wide eyes, while outside the

23

sky was filled with fast-flying birds making sharp cries of alarm.

In one, dreadful instant, the neat garden was ruined, and the cosy little home in the old hollow tree was no more. The intricate bark cupboards were crushed and broken, the box containing Cumulus's sand collection was gone for ever, and nearly all the snail shells of cordial were smashed to smithereens. And of the tree's three inhabitants there was no sign at all.

3

Endings and beginnings

After losing their home,
the Hidden Folk are forced
to set out on a quest.

Tiptoeing through the fallen branches and smashed twigs of what had once been an old ash tree came a child with unbrushed hair, wearing checked pyjamas and a dressing gown and holding half a slice of bread with much too much chocolate spread on it.

'Um . . . hello?' said Cumulus, from under an upturned birds' nest.

'Argh, help, geroff!' shouted Burnet, kicking madly to push a large twig – almost a branch! – off the spider-silk sleeping bag that had, until that moment, felt so warm and safe. Meanwhile, Moss was trying to peer through a big bunch of dry, brown ash seeds which blotted out the morning sky.

'H-has the w-w-world ended?' Moss whimpered.

Without warning, the ash seeds, known as 'keys',

were plucked up by a giant hand and tossed away as though they weighed nothing at all. Burnet, who had been about to venture over, let out a shriek and dived under the bird's nest where Cumulus was.

Moss would never forget what happened next. Looking down at the remains of their lovely home was a vast Mortal face with brown skin, black hair and chocolate spread on its chin. And it was smiling.

'Hi,' said a voice.

Eyes wide with terror, Moss froze.

'Are you injured, little person?'

How was it possible that a modern, Mortal child could speak the Wild Argot? Perhaps it was some kind of hallucination. Surely this couldn't be real!

'My name's Ro. I live next door at number fifty-one, on the other side of the fence – well, what's left of the fence. What's your name?'

'*Psssst*, Moss!' came a loud hiss from under the bird's nest. It was Burnet. 'Don't tell her your name!'

'Moss!' said the girl. 'That's a cool name. Is it short for anything?'

Sleeping bag pulled up to chin level, Moss just about managed a head-shake.

'Just Moss? OK. Well, nice to meet you – that's doing manners, my dad says, though I mostly forget to. Is there anything you need? I can probably get it for you. Like, if you ever needed sweets, I would let you have some of mine.'

Moss trembled, but didn't utter a word.

'D'you want me to put you somewhere safe for a bit, like in our shed – with the door open? That's what we did with the bird that flew into the patio doors last summer. Dad said it just needed a bit of quiet time, and he was right – it got better and flew away.'

Still Moss said nothing.

'It was a chaffinch,' said the girl. 'A male, Dad said. They live in our hedge. That's why we let it get so big – the hedge, I mean. Have you ever seen a nest? I have – an old one. It was round, with lots of soft feathers inside. I think birds are so clever to build them.'

Silence.

'I don't know why that silly chaffinch flew into the glass, though, do you? Unless he didn't notice it. I'm glad he was OK, though, even if he did poo on my scooter.'

Poor Moss hadn't blinked in what was starting to feel like days. Ro took another bite of her breakfast, and chewed, her head on one side.

'Should I . . . maybe . . . just leave you alone now?'

Moss managed a sort of nod, in slow motion.

'It's not fair – none of the animals ever want to play with me, and I only want to be friends. Will you tell them all I'm friendly? Anyway, I'm sorry about your home. It looked really cosy – even cosier than a bird's nest. Where will you go now?'

Moss shrugged. It was too upsetting to even think about that yet, especially with an actual terrifying Mortal so close by.

'Well, I hope you find a new house, and I hope it's nearby so I can visit. You should check out my garden – it's much more interesting than this one. We've got a wildflower patch and everything. OK, I'm going to get ready for school now.'

Moss let out a long, slow breath.

'Oh – before I go, would you like some of this? It's really nice. I made it.' She turned back and held out the bread, from which chocolate spread was starting to drip like delicious, brown lava.

'No? All right, then. Bye, Moss!' She grinned, took a bite of her breakfast and picked her way back to her own garden through the twigs and scattered debris of the fallen ash tree.

As soon as she was back inside, the Hidden Folk dashed into one of the flower beds where a large evergreen shrub often provided a safe place for them when they were out and about. And then they all went to pieces for several minutes, jumping up and down and shouting rude words, waving their arms about, asking one another questions but not listening to the answers, clutching their heads and generally working off the huge rush of fear and excitation that being seen by a Mortal had set off in their bodies and minds.

It's rare for a human being to catch sight of the Hidden Folk, but it has happened. For example, about a hundred years ago, two distant relatives of Burnet's, who lived in the county of Northampton-shire, were rowing a coracle along a ditch when they saw a boy in short trousers crouching in the tangled vegetation on the bank. He was gazing at them, entranced. Startled, they bent over their sycamore-seed oars and rowed hurriedly out of sight. But in the years that followed, the pair often wondered whether the boy kept what he saw a secret all his life, or had perhaps grown up to tell the story of that day.

When Moss, Cumulus and Burnet had calmed down a bit – and Moss had had a bit of a cry, which really helped – they peered out from under the bush to survey what was left of their home.

'Well, it looks like today was our lucky day,'

Cumulus said. 'We could have been really badly hurt, or even killed – if not by the tree falling down, by that Mortal just now!'

'Lucky? What do you mean, lucky?' said Moss. 'I mean, she didn't squish me or capture me for a pet – but our lovely home is gone for ever! The garden is ruined and most of our possessions are lost – including your sand collection! That doesn't feel very lucky. Oh, what shall we do? Where can we go? Whatever will become of us? And for Pan's sake, why didn't I at least say yes to some *sweets*?'

'Here's the thing I don't understand,' said Burnet. 'That child could speak the Wild Argot. I thought Mortals had forgotten how?'

'Perhaps she was a special kind of genius one,' suggested Moss.

'Yes, I suppose that must be it,' replied Burnet, 'though she didn't seem especially geniusy. For one thing, she had food all over her face.'

'I wonder . . .' said Cumulus thoughtfully. 'What if it's like playing? Every child can play, given half a chance, but the full-grown Mortals hardly ever do. Perhaps speaking the Wild Argot is the same thing – they forget how when they grow up.'

'The big ones don't play? Oh, that's sad,' said Burnet, who loved a good game of Acorn Hop.

'What do they do for fun instead?'

'Do you know, I haven't got the faintest idea,' replied Cumulus.

'Anyway, Moss, don't worry,' said Burnet reassuringly. 'Think how long we've been in the Wild World, and how many places we've lived in that time! We'll just set out for the Folly, like we discussed. Didn't we all agree it was time for a change?'

'Well . . .' said Cumulus, who didn't think they *had* quite agreed, actually. But Moss, who the night before had been the most reluctant to go on an adventure, had come around to the idea now that their ash-tree home was no more.

'Yes! Let's go straight to the Folly, today, and find our cousins. I've heard their oak tree is *extremely* sturdy,' Moss said.

'Oh, *very*,' said Burnet, giving Cumulus a nudge. 'Delightfully presented and, er, deceptively spacious!'

'Light and airy,' agreed Cumulus. 'West-facing, apparently, too.'

'Well! That's decided, then,' said Moss.

The next hour or so saw the wreckage of the ash in uproar as Moss, Cumulus and Burnet combed through the debris for anything that might have survived. They heaped up what they found in disorganized piles and generally got in one another's way, Moss stopping every so often to try and work out whether something could be glued or stitched back together and Cumulus examining every grain of sand, before casting it sadly away.

At one point the two adult Mortals who lived in the house came out and stared at the wreckage of their garden and talked to each other loudly and unintelligibly while the trio hid behind bits of broken branches. After that, Burnet began to hiss, '*Psst!* Come on!' and '*Hurry!*' every time one of them was out in the open. It was all very stressful and worrisome, and nobody was enjoying it. Eventually, Cumulus was heard to mutter an unpardonably rude word.

'Look, Burnet,' said Moss. 'We're going as fast as is creaturely possible. Why don't you go and dig a hole to hide the stuff we can't carry? If – *when* – we make it back home, we'll want our things again, and I'm not having them all stolen by shrews. You know what they're like.'

So off Burnet stamped, while Moss, with help from Cumulus, set out a nutshell bowl, catapult, carved spoon and sleeping bag each, and tried to decide how many dried grasshoppers and honey cakes they should take. Only one snail shell remained unbroken – it contained elderberry cordial, a very good vintage – and they set it aside to toast their journey.

'I've been meaning to ask,' said Cumulus. 'It looked like you were having a nightmare last night – you cried out at one stage. Do you remember?'

Moss stopped, a length of fishing line in each hand. 'Pan alive! You're right, I had a really horrible dream. I'd forgotten it until just now. I dreamt – well, I dreamt we were *all* fading away.'

'All three of us?'

'Yes, and our cousins at the Folly Brook, too, and all our kind. I know only Mortals or Mortal-made things can kill us – but in the dream we weren't being killed. We were just . . . slowly disappearing.'

'Oh, Moss, that's horrible. I'm sorry,' said Cumulus. 'Would you like a hug?'

'Yes, please,' said Moss.

Then, 'Cumulus . . .' Moss said, from inside the hug, 'it was just a bad dream, wasn't it? We're not really going to disappear?'

Over Moss's shoulder, Cumulus's face was grave. But before either of them could say anything else, Burnet reappeared and announced that the hole was ready, and that it was probably the best hole anyone had dug, ever.

'Well, you were quick!' said Moss, glad that their friend had come back in a better mood. 'However did you manage it?'

Burnet leant on a shovel newly made from a stiff, glossy holly leaf cut to shape, its tough stem the handle.

'Oh, I enlisted the help of the worms,' came the reply. 'They were ever so keen to lend a hand. Well, not a hand, of course, seeing as they don't have hands . . .' Here Burnet dissolved into snorty giggles, ended only by a sharp poke in the ribs from Cumulus.

'That was very clever of you,' said Moss.

'My joke? Yes, it was – I mean, I am,' said Burnet, with satisfaction. 'Anyway, I found a good spot and then I stamped my feet – you know, like gulls do, to make a pattering noise as though it's raining so all the worms come up to the surface. And when they did, I asked if they'd mind turning over the earth for me, to make it nice and soft, and after that I just shovelled it out!'

'And they did it for nothing?' asked Cumulus, suspiciously; earthworms are known to be unfriendly and sarcastic, and tend to keep themselves

34

to themselves.

'Oh, no, we struck a bargain. I promised them that Mr B wouldn't eat them this summer if they'd help me out.'

'Hmm. Well, just you make sure you tell him that before we leave,' Cumulus said. (Burnet forgot, of course, and there was great indignation in the worm world when Bob hoovered up three of their number the very next day.)

Once the last bundle of winter clothes, the last useful scraps of wood, the last parcel of rose petal pastry and the last pat of nut butter had been carefully wrapped up and laid in the Very Big Hole in the flower bed, and it had all been covered with tough, glossy laurel leaves and then with earth, the trio returned to the shelter of the big shrub for lunch washed down with the last of the elderberry cordial.

'Well, I'll miss our cosy home, I suppose, and the dear old garden,' said Burnet. 'But here's to adventure!' And then, after a huge swig of cordial from the snail shell, there came the sound of a burp.

'Here's to a safe journey,' said Cumulus more seriously, taking the shell in a transparent left hand and raising it to the others.

'Leave some for me!' cried Moss. But there was

only the dregs left, deep in the shell's inner spiral – and it tasted more than a little of mollusc.

The afternoon had turned bright and sunny, and warmer than it had been of late: it was a good sort of day to set out on a journey. They hoisted their packs on to their backs and said their goodbyes to their friends in the garden. The troupe of parakeets were quite cheerful about it, not having known them that long, but Whiskers the mouse and his wife Olivia cried unconsolably; Moss, Cumulus and Burnet were godparents to all their offspring, and had been to their ancestors too.

Faced with all that emotion, Spangle simply perched on the edge of the trampoline, looking casual and unbothered and letting out rhythmical clicks and bleeps with his beak shut. When it was his turn to bid the trio farewell, all he said was, 'Safe, yeah' – and off he flew. Mr B's wife Roberta presented them with a small slug each, 'to eat on the journey'; Bob, meanwhile, was coming with them a short way.

And then at last Moss, Cumulus and Burnet left the familiar patch of earth they had lived on since long before it was a garden, slipping between the wheelie bins and a brick wall out on to Ash Row. At the last moment, Moss turned around for a final look, eyes full of tears yet trying so hard to be brave – but with the old tree down it all looked so different anyway. No, there was no point in looking back. Change had found them, and they had to leave.

It was early afternoon, before home time, so there weren't any children about, and not many grown-ups either. They stuck to the inside edge of the pavement, pausing often to take shelter behind trees or garden gates and then scuttling on again, Burnet leading the way and holding up a licked finger to check the direction of the wind. Overhead, Bob flew from tree to gatepost to porch to shrub, keeping watch and warning them when to remain hidden because a Mortal was passing, pushing a rumbling baby buggy, or a cat was slinking from house to house, looking innocent but intent on catching and killing anything small. But after they had passed a couple of houses he stopped.

'I can't go any further, friends,' he called down to them at last, in his fluty whistle, where they hid under a parked car. 'This is where my territory ends, and another blackbird's begins. But if you wait a moment, I'll see if I can find you a lookout for the next part of your trip.'

He flew up to a branch of a cherry tree that was starting to put out its frilly pink blossoms. And then he looked out over the avenue with its long rows of cars and roofs and gardens, and let out a beautiful carolling song. Before long, another male blackbird appeared in the next tree and began to warble, too. But before it could turn into a singing competition, Mr B explained that he wasn't trying to come into his rival's territory and steal his food or chat up his girlfriend. He told him all about Moss, Burnet and Cumulus and their adventure, as the other bird tilted his head and looked down at them with his gold-rimmed eye. And then Bob was gone, dipping and rising over the rows of hedges and fences, back to his territory at number 52.

And so for the first part of their journey they were passed from blackbird to blackbird, all the way up the avenue to the edge of the houses. Who would ever have thought, as one bird after another broke into joyful song, that they were acting as lookouts and guides for three tiny figures slipping quietly along the pavement and leaving their home of two hundred cuckoo summers behind them – perhaps for good?

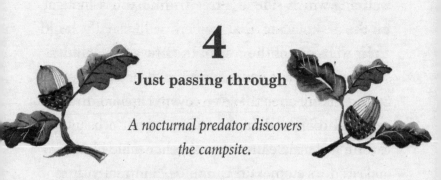

4

Just passing through

*A nocturnal predator discovers
the campsite.*

By the time it was beginning to get dark the trio had left the town behind. There were no streetlights any more and no houses or allotments; the road went past a smooth, green golf course, and not many cars drove by. They weren't in the proper countryside yet, which means farmland or wild places, but somewhere in between.

As they tramped along they all kept an eye (and an ear) out for other Hidden Folk, particularly in any spots that still felt old or wild or tangly: damp ditches, little copses, or particularly ancient trees. But none of the places they found had any of their kind looking after it – or if they were there, they weren't letting themselves be seen.

Burnet could navigate using signs in the natural world: finding the Pole Star in the night sky;

noticing which side of a tree trunk had green algae on it; or knowing that spiders will usually build their webs out of the way of the prevailing wind.

'I say we make camp in this hedge,' said Burnet now, looking about. 'We've covered a good distance today, and I'm starting to feel hungry.'

'Me too!' said Moss. 'I could eat a whole tadpole.'

'Yes, let's stop,' said Cumulus. 'I'm really tired.'

Spending the night in a tent is the most exciting thing. For starters, creating a cosy little home where there wasn't anything before makes you feel terrifically brave and as though you can do almost anything. Then there's the fun of cooking over a campfire, and eating in the open air, beneath the stars. And then the pleasure of lying in your cosy tent and listening to the sounds of the night all around you, knowing that if it rains, you'll stay snug and dry.

Of course, being outdoor creatures, most Hidden Folk are experts at camping. Although Moss, Cumulus and Burnet had been settled for a long time at Ash Row, their skills soon came back to them, and they easily pitched three little bat-skin tents, which were all but invisible amid the celandines, twining ivy and dead leaves at the base of the hedge. Moss cleared a space between the three tents for a fire, making sure that nothing nearby could accidentally catch alight, and Burnet went off to look for cheesy-bobs (their name for woodlice), which were something of a delicacy. Hidden Folk – particularly when they're on the road – like to roll them in clay and cook them in the ashes of the fire, like tiny baked potatoes.

Along the base of the hedge was litter that had been thrown out of car windows: juice boxes, a take-away carton and several sweet wrappers, none of which would ever rot away but would be there for ever, because they were plastic. It seemed clear that the hedge didn't have a caretaker. There was even a pair of boy's nylon underpants with superheroes on them. Being a practical sort, Burnet wondered whether they could be used to make anything, like a parachute, or the sail of a boat. But no – it probably wasn't a good idea. They didn't look entirely clean.

Not far away was a tree stump with a crevice in it, and in the crevice was a stash of hazelnuts. They had been stored there last autumn by a bank vole, who had been caught and eaten one frosty day by a russet-backed kestrel called Skyhover. They were soon added to Burnet's backpack, along with eleven unfortunate woodlice who had been sheltering under the leaf litter and nibbling bits of rotting wood.

Once they had all had their fill of slow-baked cheesy-bobs, Moss threw some earth on the fire to make sure it was safely out. Then they crawled into their tents and got into their sleeping bags. Before long, loud snores began to issue from Burnet's tent, but in the others, tiny eyes still gleamed in the darkness: two in Moss's tent, and one in Cumulus's.

'C-Cumulus,' came a shaky whisper from Moss's tent. 'Cumulus, are you awake?'

'Yes, Moss. Are you feeling homesick?'

'I am a bit.'

Quietly, so as not to wake Burnet, Cumulus crawled into Moss's tent.

'I feel a bit like when I had to leave my meadow,' whispered Moss, sadly. 'I know I didn't look after it for as long as you did your pond, but my heart was broken for a hundred cuckoo summers. It feels as if it still is, sometimes.'

'I know,' said Cumulus. 'We all still love the Wild World, even though we're not caretakers any more. And I miss Ash Row too.'

'Do you think we'll ever go back?'

'Who knows. But just think, after you lost your meadow, you made friends with Burnet and found that nice row of ash trees to live in, didn't you? And later I came along. We may not have jobs any more, but at least we have each other. And we three will always be friends, you know? Until for ever.'

Moss managed a tiny smile. 'Thanks, Cumulus.'

'That's all right. Now, I'm going to tell you something, because I need to share my worries, too. But you're not to tell anyone, or make a fuss?'

Moss felt very flattered. It was nice to be trusted, and to feel useful, too.

'All right. What is it?'

'It's . . . well, it's my hand.'

'The invisible one, or the other one?'

Cumulus held one hand up to Moss's face in the dimness. This time it wasn't the left one, but the right.

'That's just it. Look.'

'I can't see anything.'

'I know. That's the point.'

'Oh, Cumulus,' whispered Moss, blinking back tears. They had a hug, and Cumulus promised there was no need to worry, but it still took Moss ages to get to sleep.

In the darkest dead of night all three suddenly sat up in their separate tents, eyes wide, unsure what had woken them. Cautiously, they peeked out of their tent flaps to whisper to one another: '*Pssst*, are you awake?' 'Did you hear something?' 'Yes, I heard it too!'

There was no moon, only the distant lights of the town visible amid the blackness, but Hidden Folk can see quite well in the dark and there was no visible danger nearby. Though last year's dry, russet leaves clinging to the hedge rattled a bit spookily, they could hear no Mortals or smell no Mortal smell. But there was definitely something – or someone – close to them: all three distinctly felt they were no longer alone.

The sound that had woken them came again, from somewhere above: a sharp '*Ke-WICK!*' – answered by a long, wavering '*Whoo-hooo-ooo*' from a little further away. Then a brown owl with a heart-shaped face and beautiful mottled feathers detached itself from the beech tree that hung over the road and landed at the base of the hedge.

'Now, what in all the Wild World are you three?' said the owl, peering at them. 'I can see you're not voles, which is a shame, because I'm hungry. Are you goblins?'

Cumulus, Burnet and Moss all bristled. 'Absolutely *not*,' said Cumulus. 'We are Hidden

Folk. And you, I believe, are a tawny owl.'

'That's right! I'm Mrs Ben . . . *Ke-WICK*!' she cried again, swivelling her head a little eerily to the right and waiting for the answering '*Whooo*'. 'And over there's my other half – he's a bit shy. Oo-oo, Hidden Folk, are you? Very interesting. I've heard tell about you in stories, but you three are the very first of your kind I've ever seen. To be honest, I thought you were extinct!'

'Extinct?' Cumulus frowned. 'Oh, no, that's not possible. Our kind are immortal – we'll be in the Wild World for ever. Extinct? Pan alive, no.'

Burnet spoke up. 'Are there really none of our kind living in these parts, then? None at all?'

'Not that I know of, I'm afraid, and I'm sure I would. Are you passing through, or here to stay? I must say, I'd love to have you on my patch – it's said that your kind are lucky, you know. Once I've finished hunting, I could scout around for a burrow for you, if you like; I don't mind flying on for a little while after it begins to get light.'

'Oh – we're on our way to visit our distant relations at the Folly Brook,' said Burnet. 'But thank you very much, it's very kind of you. Do you know how much further we have to go?'

Mrs Ben's eyes went a little bulgy, and Moss and

Cumulus gave one another a worried look. But after a moment she stood up very tall, closed her eyes, opened her beak and deposited a small, neat parcel on the grass. It was a pellet of grey fur, scrupulously clean bones and other indigestible parts of the most recent things she'd eaten – vole's skulls, mouse vertebra, shiny beetle wings and even a frog's jawbone. Moss took a step back, but Burnet gazed at it in fascination.

'Pardon me,' Mrs Ben said, returning to her usual height and blinking her great eyes twice. 'Hmm, the Folly Brook . . . I believe a distant ancestor of mine once lived in a tree on the bank of the stream there – you know how these stories are handed down through the generations. But it's ever such a long way away, you know. I couldn't say exactly where it is, only that you won't get there on foot before winter comes, oo-ooh, no, not a chance.'

Burnet's plan had been to ask the birds for help, and here was the first one they'd met, one who flew much further than the blackbirds or sparrows, and she wasn't able to help them on their way. It was all very well being able to tell north from south, and navigate by the stars, but you still needed to know which direction you ought to be heading in – and how long it was likely to take.

Cumulus turned to Burnet. 'I knew it! It's just too far to walk at the pace we go. We're too small.'

Moss looked anxiously from one to the other. Sometimes they got annoyed with each other, which always felt uncomfy. Once, Burnet had kicked Cumulus's shin during a heated argument about whether they could keep a dung beetle as a pet, and Cumulus had fallen on the beetle and squished it. While that had solved the problem in one way, the pair had refused to speak to each other for nearly ten whole cuckoo summers. It had been a very frustrating time indeed.

Mrs Ben raised a foot rather inelegantly and scratched herself under the beak with one talon. 'Well, if you need to go far, you could always try the deer,' she said. 'They're fast, and kind to those they consider friends – though I can't guarantee that they'll trust you, oo-ooh, no, I can't guarantee it at all. But if you're polite and treat them with respect, they might be persuaded take you at least part of the way.'

'That's a terrific idea!' said Moss. 'Don't you agree – Burnet, Cumulus? Gosh, I would never have thought of that.'

'I would have, if anyone had thought to ask me,' sniffed Burnet, which made Cumulus's eyebrows shoot up in surprise.

'Well, anyway,' said Moss hurriedly, before the two of them got into an argument, 'that's settled. Can you tell us where to find them?'

'Oo-oh, no – not off the top of my head, I'm afraid. Deer are ever so secretive, even though there are so many of them, and the herds do rather move about. But if you meet me here at the same time tomorrow night, I'll bring news if I can. And in the meantime, you might as well ask the other creatures here for directions to the Folly Brook. Just don't bother with the voles – they're terribly dim. And so easy to catch!'

And with that she spread her wings and lofted up into the black night sky, only a final '*Ke-wick*!' and answering '*Whoooo*' fading away to the east.

Have you ever been awake and outdoors when the sun comes up in spring? What happens is this: all the birds sing as loudly as they can, at the same time, to welcome the new day in. And none of your footling, half-hearted chirping, either: no, this is the real deal, the full whack, the bees' knees, like an orchestra or a choir, or a football crowd when there's a goal, all of them giving it their utmost – plump thrushes shouting, tiny wrens trilling like they'll burst at any moment, robins sad and silvery, blackbirds joyful, wood warblers spinning pennies, chaffinch songs all bouncy, blackcaps giving it welly, dunnocks sounding scratchy, starlings wolf-whistling and beeping like robots, and all manner of other lovely melodies. That's what the Hidden Folk woke up to that morning, and while they were well used to the dawn chorus back at Ash Row, now they were heading into the countryside there were a lot more birds, and some different ones, too, whose songs were less familiar, and the whole shebang was so exciting that there was absolutely no going back to sleep.

After a quick breakfast of popped pollen and freshly squeezed dandelion squash, they decided to strike out and explore their surroundings. It had been getting dark when they set up camp and none of them had had much of a look at where they actually were. Cars were starting to pass by on the road by the hawthorn hedge, so they headed in the other direction, into some long grass still wet with morning dew.

Down at ground level, tiny paths wound this way and that through the tall stems. They were invisible to anyone looking down on the field from above, though they could be detected by birds of prey like kestrels. The paths had been made by the Field People – voles, mice and shrews – but you'd have to be as small as the Hidden Folk to use them. Burnet went first, swinging the 'Stanley' knife about like a machete to clear the way, but taking care not to harm any of the bright green spiders, shield bugs or crane flies that lived in the damp grass. It really was hard going – a bit like a jungle, in fact, with sticky goosegrass, golden buttercups and delicate, lilac cuckooflowers growing thickly between the stems and tangling everything up. The grass itself was made up of several species, many of which had wonderful names like sweet vernal, red fescue, crested dogstail and Yorkshire fog.

Imagine you're a wood pigeon perched in a tree and looking down at the scene. There's a hawthorn hedge between the road and the field; it's a bit straggly and gappy, and there are dead bits and litter, because it hasn't been properly cared for by Mortals, but it's alive and is just coming into leaf. At the base of the hedge are three bat-skin tents that look just like dead leaves, and the blackened remnants of a tiny fire. A few feet away a patch of long, green grass is moving ever so slightly, but not with the breeze – and the movement is travelling further into the field. You can't see the three Hidden Folk at all, because the tall grass has closed over their heads, but you can mark their progress, just about, if you know what to look for.

And then you see another movement in the grass, a little way away; a fluid movement undulating towards them. And your bird's heart jumps with fear in your feathered breast because you know what it is: you've seen that kind of motion in the long grass before, and you realize—

'Snake!' came a sudden cry from the long grass as a wood pigeon took off with a clatter from the trees and flew off in alarm. It was Burnet, steel 'Stanley' blade held aloft and catching the sun.

5

The confrontation

*The trio encounter a
smooth-talking character.*

Deep amid the long grass in a green field by a road a confrontation was taking place, totally hidden from the Mortals zooming past in cars on their way to school and work and the shops. Even if they were going slowly enough, most Mortals have no idea about the secret world of wild creatures – and of course the things you don't believe in are particularly hard to see.

An olive-green snake had stopped his sinuous progress through the grass stalks. Head raised, he regarded the three Hidden Folk before him with beautiful, expressionless eyes.

'Aargh!' shouted Burnet as loudly as possible, waving 'Stanley' around randomly. '*Aaaarrrrgh!*'

Moss let out a little whimper and tried unsuccessfully to grab hold of Cumulus's hand. The desire to turn and run was almost overwhelming, but if everything turned out all right, such cowardice would be very hard to live down.

'Burnet!' hissed Cumulus. 'Use your words! Snakes can understand the Wild Argot, just like everything else, you know.'

'Oh! Er, yes, of course,' said Burnet a little sheepishly. 'Well, you – you just *stay back*, all right, mister? As you can see, we're well armed!'

'Oh. I'm dreadfully thorry to have thtartled you,' came the reply. The grass snake lowered his fine, enamelled head and looked a little glum. 'I jutht don't know why everyone's tho very frightened of me. I thwear I haven't eaten anyone I thouldn't have in *monththssss.*'

At this, Cumulus stepped forward. 'We're very pleased to make your acquaintance. My name is Cumulus. I'm sorry about my friend here; we were just a little thtartled, that's all. *Startled*, I mean.'

'Please, call me *Thven*,' the snake hissed. 'And you are . . . ?'

Looking a little shamefaced, Burnet and Moss introduced themselves. Of course, they had met snakes many times before in their long lives, but not for some time, and while they all knew that the ones who live on these islands are shy and

53

peaceable beings, the fact that they moved so differently to other animals could give the unwary a bit of a fright. But one must never judge anyone or anything by appearances, which is why Burnet and Moss felt that they had rather let themselves down. To complicate matters, Burnet was wearing a snakeskin waistcoat, and felt very self-conscious about it.

'I only woke up from hibernation a few dayth ago, and I'm feeling rather peckith,' said Sven. 'I don't thuppose any of you know where I might obtain some *eggth*?'

Moss's tummy rumbled. It wasn't long since they'd had breakfast, but the Hidden Folk prize an egg over almost any other food, and in the wild they can only be found in spring.

'I'm afraid not, but we could offer you a dried grasshopper if that would help at all,' Moss said.

'Ick! Horrible thingth,' the snake replied. 'Thorry – that'th a very kind offer, but they do rather thtick in the throat if one can't *chew*' – and he opened his pink mouth very wide to show them that he had no back molars at all, and no venomous fangs either, only some tiny, backward-pointing teeth to help him hold on to wriggly things like frogs without them getting away.

'Erm, well, we should really be getting on,' said

Burnet, who was feeling slightly peculiar about all those teeth – no matter how harmless Sven was.

'Well, do be careful, won't you? There's a Mortalth road over there for all their thmelly chariots to roar along. I thouldn't go near it, if I were you – thoo many creatures never come back. If I were you, I'd thtay here in the grathy field. Or if you mutht travel, you could vithit the wood over *there*' (he rose a little and gestured with his head). 'Oh! And next to it is a ditch which *thometimes* hath frog-thpawn in it, though not often enough these dayth. Very *tathty*!' he concluded, with a happy hiss. 'Now, may I athk you thomething before you go?'

'Absolutely,' said Burnet.

The snake nodded towards Cumulus. 'You, the old one. Where have your *handth* gone?'

'Oh. Ah, yes. So the thing is . . .' began Cumulus.

'Wait,' interrupted Burnet. 'Handth, as in two? As in . . . both?'

'Yes, well, about that . . .'

'Show me!'

Cumulus held up both hands, which weren't there.

'But this is awful! This is terrifying! Moss, did you know about this?'

Moss looked down.

'And exactly when were you going to tell me?' demanded Burnet.

But just before the quarrel had a chance to develop, something strange began to happen to Sven. His eyes turned milky and blue, and he became very still. Then the skin of his head began to split open, but underneath, healthy new scales could be seen. Quickly, a brand new head emerged, and – Pan alive! – he was so handsome, his chin even whiter and the markings at the back of his head even brighter than before.

'*Excuthe* me for just one moment,' he said, and, closing his eyes in bliss, he began to rub his long flanks against the young stems of cow parsley and other plants nearby. Slowly, an entire layer of dead skin peeled off, inside-out like a sock, to be left amid the grass, a treasure for anyone who might be lucky enough to come across it. At last, the entire metre-long length of him emerged, his olive-green scales gleaming in the spring sunshine.

'*Thath* better!' he said, and began to slither away. 'Do you know, I've been wanting to do that ever thince I woke up. Goodbye, now! Hope you have a nithe day!'

Once Sven had gone, the three of them sat down under a clump of ribwort plantain to talk things through. At first Cumulus insisted that a person's health was a private matter, so Burnet had no right to be cross, but Burnet pointed out that Moss had been told that the disappearing was getting worse, and added that not being told felt like being left out, and perhaps not mattering to anyone at all.

'You do matter! Of course you matter!' said Cumulus.

'Well, if that's true, tell me honestly: why confide in Moss, and not in me?'

'Honestly? Well, because I didn't want you to overreact. The truth is that Moss is – well, Moss is a better listener than you.'

'What! How dare you!' spluttered Burnet. 'That's a really hurtful thing to say. What a nasty, mean person you are.'

'You see, this is exactly what I—'

'Oh, is someone speaking?' said Burnet, haughtily, with folded arms. 'I'm sorry, I can't hear a thing.'

'Oh, Burnet, please don't do this,' said Moss. 'You're both my friends, and—'

'No, no, it's quite all right, Moss. Please don't trouble yourself to explain it to me. I'm absolutely, *perfectly* fine.'

Of course, Burnet wasn't fine at all, but sulking: a way of trying to win an argument without using your words to say what you're really upset about. It's an underhand tactic that means nothing gets properly talked through, and it can really come between people who otherwise love each other very much. Both Cumulus and Moss found it terribly hard, though, to be fair, Burnet had been making an effort not to sulk since the infamous dung beetle row.

'Burnet,' said Cumulus, 'if you want people to tell you things, you have to listen to them without reacting badly. That means not panicking, or sulking, or taking things personally. Which you are doing right now.'

But Burnet, feeling under attack, couldn't see the truth in what Cumulus was saying, and stamped off in a huff.

A little glumly, Cumulus and Moss set out to explore the field, the shady wood which would soon be carpeted in bluebells, and the ditch, which was overgrown and blocked, so that it only had a little bit of water in it and no newts or frogspawn at all.

'I certainly don't think that ditch has a guardian,' said Cumulus as they tramped past. 'It doesn't look very well looked-after at all!'

The sun was warm and the sky was blue, and from all around came the calls of birds as the year's new couples talked to one another about which tree to build a nest in and where the juiciest caterpillars might be found once they had their chicks. There were the wheezy tweets of blue tits and great tits calling, '*TEA-cher! TEA-cher*'. From the little wood came the '*Dink! Dink! Dink! Dink! Dink!*' of a chiff-chaff who had flown in all the way from Africa, a journey of six thousand miles. He was the first of the summer visitors to return, having spent the winter eating insects in warm, sub-Saharan weather; but come spring there were more bugs to eat here than in Africa, so he had returned to start a family. He was hoping that some female chiff-chaffs would soon arrive.

Everything, it seemed, was suddenly growing. After the long months of winter, when the world felt so still and cold and dead, all the plants and trees were coming alive, pushing their stems upwards, sending roots downwards, or unfurling fresh new leaves. The air smelt green and delicious, early bumblebees were emerging from hibernation, and for the first time in months there were insects crawling and flying about – which was good for all the birds and other creatures that relied on them, including the Hidden Folk. They tended not to eat butterflies or moths (though some caterpillars were extremely tasty), but Burnet was handy with a catapult and could take down a dragonfly from a good two metres away.

After filling a frogskin pouch with water from the ditch, the pair returned to their campsite, where Moss set about making wild carrot stew with thyme dumplings in an aluminium cauldron that had once – although they didn't know it – held a tea light candle. Cumulus disappeared for a rest, and after a little while Burnet came back, looking a little bit sheepish, having got the better of the sulk.

'Hello, Moss. I've been out on a recce,' Burnet said.

'Oh, yes?' said Moss, adding a couple of aromatic fennel seeds to the pot. 'What did you discover?'

'I had a really good look but I couldn't find any Hidden Folk at all here – just as Mrs Ben said. Zero. Zilch. Not a one.'

'That's a bit odd, isn't it? You'd expect one or two, at least.'

'I'm going to tell Cumulus. But first, Moss . . . I wanted to say sorry – to both of you. I just felt a bit left out, and it stung. But because of that, I went and made it all about myself, when it's not even me who's poorly – which is *exactly* why Cumulus chose to confide in you and not me in the first place! I'm really cross with myself.'

Moss smiled. Burnet was doing a very brave thing, and deserved a lot of kindness and admiration at that moment. It's not at all easy to haul yourself out of a bad mood, and it can be even harder to apologize.

'Why don't you and Cumulus have a good talk,' Moss replied kindly. 'Don't worry, I'll keep your dinner warm.'

The two old friends soon made up. Then, having apologized, Burnet asked how Cumulus felt about the fading getting worse.

'And you're sure it doesn't hurt, or anything?'

'Not at all,' replied Cumulus. 'I feel all right in myself. It's just that – well, I know we're the Hidden Folk, but I wouldn't like to become *completely* invisible, you know?'

'Wouldn't you? Oh, I would! I'd sneak around and spy on people. I'd have to take all my clothes off, though, or I'd just be a kilt and waistcoat floating around – that would be odd!'

'That's all very well, but I'd hate to think none of my friends would be able to see me ever again,' explained Cumulus. 'Even if they knew I was there, they wouldn't really be looking *at* me, not properly. It would be . . . well, I'd feel I didn't exist any more. I'd be – *unseen*.'

That was a sobering thought. 'Well, the only thing for it is to get to the Folly as quickly as possible, and ask our cousins for help,' said the ever-practical Burnet. 'Surely Dodder will know what to do – and perhaps where the rest of our kind have got to as well.'

Cumulus and Burnet emerged from the tent firm friends again, and then they all sat cross-legged around the fire eating warm, fragrant stew from hazelnut shells. Overhead, the pale sky became opalescent, like the inside of an oyster shell, and the sun sank lower and lower in the west until it was behind the trees on the horizon. Little by little, the light began to fade.

In the soundless way of all owls, Mrs Ben materialized on the ground nearby and folded her great wings tidily behind her.

'Go-ooo-ood evening, all,' she began. 'I bring news of the deer herd. They're not far away, and they're willing to meet you. But they leave tonight, at star-rise – can you be ready?'

Moss looked at the others, heart thumping, though whether in fear or excitement it was hard to tell.

'Well, that's terrific news!' said Burnet. 'Of course we can. Saddle me up!'

'They'll take us?' said Cumulus, whose long hair glimmered white in the evening dimness.

'As to that, I couldn't say. I managed to speak to one very briefly. I got the feeling she had heard of your kind, and was curious to meet you. But it wasn't easy to talk, they're so wary of everyone – including us owls.'

'Imagine that,' said Burnet, who was more than a little wary of the big bird of prey, too.

'You must cross the field, heading north. Over the stream, you'll find yourself in a wood carpeted in the young leaves of wild garlic – you can't miss the smell. Carry straight on until you reach another field, with young wheat in it. Turn east and follow the ditch to the corner. That's where they gather. You must speak quietly and respectfully, and show yourselves worthy of their trust.'

Cumulus stood up and bowed. 'I don't know how to thank you, Mrs Ben. You've done us a great service. Will we see you again?'

'Perhaps, on your way back – if you come back!

63

I'll be sure to look out for you,' she said, and then she opened her huge tawny wings and took off. 'Goo-*hoo-hoood* luck!' came a faint cry from the orange and gold sky overhead.

6

By the light of the stars

*Our intrepid explorers must
persuade the gentle deer
to trust them.*

It didn't take the three of them long to get ready,
and then Burnet led the way into the tangled
grass and across the dark field.

'How do you know which way's north?' whispered Moss.

'Easy,' replied Burnet. 'Where did the sun rise this morning?'

'I can't remember.'

Burnet tutted. 'All right, then, where did it set just now?'

'Oh! Over there.' Moss pointed to where the horizon still held a faint glow.

'Now, we know the sun rises in the east and sets in the west, don't we? So . . .'

'It goes *north, east, south, west* . . .' muttered Moss. 'So that makes this way north!'

65

'Exactly,' said Burnet. 'Easy when you know how.'

They listened for the sound of running water and crossed the stream on an old plank bridge, then followed their noses to the wood of wild garlic. From there they found a field of young, green wheat that had been sown in rows last September. They were surprised to find that it had no wild flowers or harvest mice living in it. It seemed very different to the wheat fields of the past.

When they arrived at the corner of the field, the evening star – the planet Venus – was glimmering brightly in the night sky. As they waited for the deer to arrive, bats flickered past. At one point a cluster of tiny blinking lights passed slowly over-head accompanied by a soft, mechanical roar. In recent decades they had become used to aeroplanes, and had learnt to ignore them. If only the Mortals overhead, eating meals on plastic trays or dozing with their headphones on, could have seen what was happening on the ground far, far below! Then they would have realized that the world was a very different place than they had ever realized.

'*Brrrr*,' said Moss, giving a little shiver. The spring night was actually quite warm, but nerves can often make you feel jumpy. In the darkness

Burnet shifted from foot to foot, impatiently; only Cumulus remained still.

And then there they were, materializing one by one from the shadows: a herd of fallow does whose big, dark eyes gleamed in the starlight, and who had managed to encircle them without making a sound. Moss, Burnet and Cumulus found themselves surrounded as the deer stretched their necks down to gaze at them and blew gently through soft nostrils, their warm breath scented with grass and bark and flowers.

Burnet and Moss bowed in all directions, Burnet snatching off Moss's acorn-cup hat, but Cumulus knelt down humbly, and after a moment the other two followed suit. Although the deer were big, they were such shy and beautiful animals it felt a great privilege that they had chosen to come so close.

'Are you the creatures that seek our help?' came a low voice.

'We are, ma'am,' replied Cumulus, head bowed.

'You are . . . Hidden Folk? Truly?'

'Yes. Are we the first you've ever met?'

There was some murmuring among the does as they conferred with one another. Dozens of dark eyes regarded them with growing interest.

'We know of your kind only from old tales and

legends,' said the doe. 'We understand that once your job was to look after the Wild World, each with your little acre, and that at long last Mortals deposed you, hundreds of cuckoo summers ago. But that is all.'

'We definitely are – Hidden Folk, I mean,' said Burnet. 'All three of us. You can tell.'

There came quiet laughter. 'Yes, we can see that now. May we know your names?'

Moss, who had just nudged Burnet very hard in the ribs, spoke up. 'I'm Moss, ma'am, and this is Cumulus, and my friend here is Burnet.'

'I am Fleet, and these are my sisters, my elders, my daughters and cousins.'

'We're honoured to make your acquaintance,' said Moss.

'One of you is . . . afflicted,' came the gentle voice. 'What form does this affliction take?'

'Oh. It's me,' said Cumulus miserably, standing up and holding both invisible hands out. 'But I kept my hands behind me. How did you know?'

'We deer notice everything. It is how we survive.' Then she bent her beautiful head to Cumulus and gently inhaled.

'This fading . . . it is not a sickness,' she said.

'But – what is it, then?' said Burnet.

68

'I can only tell you what I know, which is that your friend is not ill in body. Something else is happening, something . . . unusual. You would do well to find out what it is – and soon.'

The three Hidden Folk looked at one another. It was the first time any of them had let themselves feel really, truly frightened by what was happening to Cumulus – and what might happen to them all.

'But to the matter at hand,' continued Fleet. 'What ails you is no danger to the herd, so we are willing to carry you into the wild countryside. But there are two conditions: firstly, you must eat as we do, and cast away now anything you carry that was once living. We are of the hunted, and because of this we cannot bear to see any creature eaten that has known life.'

A little reluctantly, all three shrugged off their backpacks and opened them up. They took out all the dried grasshoppers and baked woodlice they carried, and Moss pulled out three kippered stickle-backs kept for a special feast. Around them, the deer drew back as one from the smoked fish smell; quickly, so as not to further offend them, Moss plucked some thick blades of fresh grass and covered the pile of food.

'Secondly, you must not speak for the entire

journey: not a word, for wolves have sharp ears. We will speak to you if and when it is safe to do so; and if you fail to keep silent we will part company immediately, leaving you to continue alone. The tales we have heard describe you as a talkative people; is this a condition you can accept?'

All three nodded firmly. It was true that they could be chatterboxes among themselves, but, unlike Mortals, the Hidden Folk also know how to be quiet. What's more, when they go fishing, or hunting grasshoppers, they often use gestures to communicate with one another. Staying silent for a few hours would be easy, they all believed.

Burnet raised a hand. 'Please, ma'am . . . you mentioned wolves. I didn't think there were any left here – not for a good while now.'

There came a quiet murmuring from the herd.

'You are not the first to tell us that may be so,' replied Fleet. 'And yet – how is it possible for an animal to just disappear? Wolves are our foes, it's true, and always have been; but they have a right to life, just as we do – and as you do, too. They are part of the great perfection of the Wild World; how could they cease to exist? Surely Pan would not allow it to be so.'

'Well, instead of becoming extinct, perhaps they

just went . . . somewhere else? Somewhere a long way away?' suggested Burnet.

'Perhaps. But we can take no chances. The fear of them is rooted deep within us, as is all wild creatures' fear of Mortalkind. And in any case, we believed the river engineers – the beavers – had left these shores, but then another herd brought word of them from the west. And we have not seen any Hidden Folk for a long while, yet here you are, Pan be praised. Who is to say it may not be the same with wolves?'

'Can't argue with that,' shrugged Burnet.

'Before we set out, may I ask you something?' said Moss.

'You may,' murmured Fleet.

'How long is the journey? Will we be there by morning?'

'No, Moss.'

'By dinner time tomorrow?'

She dipped her head, and her dark eyes shone in the starlight. 'We move after dark, and rest in the daytime. All being well, you will be travelling with us for many nights.'

7

Passengers

A great distance is travelled.

Years later, whenever Moss tried to describe in any detail their exhausting, otherworldly, seemingly endless journey with the fallow herd, it would feel as though there were no words to capture its strangeness – perhaps because words were forbidden them for so many days and nights that they stopped thinking in language and began to just be, existing in the flow of the moment as only wild creatures can.

However many times the story was told in later years, Moss never found the perfect words to describe what it had really felt like to grip the coarse, dun coat of a doe at her muscled neck, to hold on tight as she stepped carefully, swaying a little from side to side; to not be able to see your companions, each on their own mount, lost somewhere in the darkness; the sudden halts, when the deer's big ears would swivel alertly and you could feel the blood thump warm in her veins; the times when the does would encounter other deer and greet them in the dimness, or regard them from a distance, warily; the terrifying seconds when, as one, the herd would flee through the dark tree trunks or leap across unlit roads as you held on tight for dear life, arms aching, hoping against hope that you would not be shaken free to fly through the air and land with a thump under stampeding hooves. It was exhausting and terrifying and wonderful, all at the same time.

One of the hardest things was being separated from the others, and just having to trust that they were all right. To feel less worried, Moss would think up rhymes that might work in the annual ballad, and imagined reciting them to their friends in Ash Row should they ever return. It would definitely need some extra verses describing their adventures – how brave the others would think them for travelling all this way! And then there were the legendary stories and songs of the Hidden Folk, composed who knows how many cuckoo summers ago by ancestors who were proper poets and famous writers. Moss knew many of them off by heart.

As the sun rose in the east each morning, the dawn chorus daily growing louder as more and more of the warm-weather birds arrived, the deer would look for somewhere to lie up amid the young bracken or long grass. Then Fleet would seek out the does who carried Cumulus and Burnet so that the three of them could rest together in silence, making conker fritters from their flour, nibbling on bits of bracket fungus Burnet foraged from the trunks of trees, and drinking dew. Sometimes Cumulus wandered off alone for a little bit, and the others knew their friend was checking to see if the disappearing had got any worse. Then they would wait anxiously until they were reunited, and make a cosy space between them so they could all rest against the does' soft, warm flanks as they chewed the cud. Sometimes they could feel the does' fawns moving gently around inside them, dappled bundles of legs and ears and eyelashes waiting to be born.

They often saw rabbits, who came out of their burrows at dawn and dusk to eat grass while the dew was still on it and it was nice and moist. There is a long-standing friendship between deer and rabbits, and the herd also had great respect for their cousins the hares – beautiful, mysterious and solitary, with their piston-powered limbs, long ears and golden eyes.

But because the deer travelled at night, and were so shy in their habits, they rarely saw any Mortals; and Mortals almost never saw the deer, either, despite the great numbers of their kind that lived in the woods and grazed the field margins. When they encountered any, the herd would freeze, and then melt away silently before they could be seen.

Only once during their journey was a Mortal aware of their passage through the spring countryside. Early one evening Moss looked up from Fleet's back to see a short-haired woman with a black-and-white dog standing quietly at the edge of the wood. She was lowering what looked like a pair of small black tubes from her eyes, and she was smiling at them – just like the little girl Ro had smiled. Fleet gazed back at her warily for a long moment before the herd turned as one, stepped into the shadows, and disappeared.

'I sense you are troubled, Moss,' Fleet murmured the next morning, when they had found somewhere safe to rest for the day.

Moss nodded, and Cumulus sat up to listen, too.

'What is it?' asked Fleet gently. 'You may speak.'

'I was thinking about that Mortal we saw yesterday evening. I was wondering, are they all bad? Even the ones who smile, and look friendly?'

'Not at all. They often harm the Wild World, knowingly and unknowingly – but that's only because they don't realize we are their brothers and sisters. Just imagine how lonely that must be.'

'Lonely?' asked Moss. 'With so many of them? How so?'

'Fleet's right,' said Cumulus quietly. 'Yes, they have each other, and they seem to like to cluster together – like starlings, I suppose, or honey bees. But wherever Mortals go, everything flees from them: the deer and the songbirds, the harvest mice and hares, the fish in the streams – even the butterflies. They come into a wild place, and it empties. They can never, ever meet and talk to other creatures, as we do. They don't have any friends, except themselves.'

'That Mortal we saw the other day had an animal companion – a dog she kept fastened to her by a red rope.'

'A pet, yes – an unwild thing,' said Fleet. 'I think that must be why Mortals created them: it helps them feel less alone in the Wild World. Always being run from – that is a terrible burden to bear.'

One warm afternoon, when it had begun to seem as though they had been travelling for ever – and when their stores of honey cake were almost gone – Fleet came back from grazing and lowered her head to where the three Hidden Folk sat quietly among a haze of bluebells.

Although they had been alone for some time that day, the herd away grazing, Moss and Cumulus hadn't spoken a word to one another, because the habit of gesturing and nodding had become so strong. Even Burnet had so far managed not to break their vow of silence, which had surprised everyone.

'Little friends,' Fleet murmured, 'are you in good health and good spirits?'

They nodded and smiled up at her. The smell of the bluebells was intoxicating.

'We set out at dusk. This part of the route contains grave dangers – for all of us. Make sure you are at peace with Pan, and with each other, before we set out.'

That evening, Moss, Cumulus and Burnet prepared for their last, perilous ride with the deer. As usual, Fleet woke them up by breathing softly on them, and as they rubbed the sleep from their eyes she bent first her forelegs and then her hind legs until her pale belly touched the ground. Backpack shouldered, Moss took hold of the longer, shaggier hair at her shoulder and used it to climb up her flank and perch at the back of her neck. When Burnet and Cumulus had also clambered up on to their does, the deer stood, and the herd gathered quietly around them in the dusk. The three friends looked long at one another; even Burnet seemed serious, and didn't pull a face or mess about.

The herd began to move, each doe stepping at her own pace into the darkness between the trees, choosing her own path but remaining constantly aware of the others. They passed silently through a dark, endless conifer plantation with brown, dry pine needles underfoot, then emerged to skirt the edges of fields. Some were planted with barley, which was young enough still to look like grass in the moonlight; one or two were scattered with remnants of fodder beet, grown by Mortals for livestock like sheep to graze in wintertime.

After many hours a gentle breeze got up in the

darkness and wandered restlessly around the dim fields and the woods and farms, gathering the scent of spring blossom and the light kiss of dew, stirring the colts in the paddocks so that they switched their tails and stamped, raising the heads of the ewes and their sleeping lambs, chasing the owls and the bats to their roosting-places, and bringing the silent herd to a halt, nostrils twitching, in the heart of a meadow deep in the countryside. The deer breathed in the breeze, and it told them three things: dawn was rising somewhere far away below the dark horizon; there was moving water somewhere in the distance; and closer, much closer, was the terrible danger Fleet had spoken of: a wide, busy road that smelt of tarmac and diesel and death.

The sky was beginning to lighten when the herd finally reached the top of the sloping embankment. Moss gazed down in dismay at the hard surface along which the Mortals' chariots thundered: small ones and enormous ones, blazing with lights, white at the front and red at the back. All along it, pressed into its black surface, were the remains of their fellow creatures, and Moss tried not to look because it was too, too horrible to recognize them and know how they had died. A few yards away Burnet's face was turned away from the carnage, too; only

Cumulus gazed straight ahead at the roaring, flood-lit death-route, a single tear glinting in the rising light.

And then, without warning, one of the leading does leapt down the embankment, found a gap in the traffic and was across the road in three bounds, disappearing into the scrubby trees on the other side. Then they all surged, for a herd must always stay together, and when one starts to cross a road they will all follow, for good or for ill, each hoping that the gap between the death-chariots holds long enough for them to get safely to the other side. Moss felt Fleet's muscles bunch as she prepared to leap; it was just enough warning to grip hard with hands and thighs before she leapt down the slope to the tarmac, her sisters and elders and daughters before her and behind, and then they rode on, on, *on* into the thundering maelstrom of cars.

There was a pleasant, restful sound of a breeze stirring the young ash leaves and making them whisper. Over it floated the songs of birds, some close and some more distant, greeting the bright new dawn.

Eyes closed, head spinning, Moss heard these things as though in a dream, and only slowly realized that they were real. Had they made it, at last? Was this the Folly Brook – or was it heaven? Were they still in the Wild World, or had Pan called them home?

Slowly, and with a thumping head, Moss sat up and looked around. Cumulus was sitting nearby, wrapped in a sycamore leaf and looking pale, while further away, at the edge of a hazel thicket, stood the herd of deer. They were all looking away, back in the direction of the distant motorway; all appeared tense, with their ears swivelled forward.

'What's happened? How did we get here?' asked Moss; but Cumulus didn't answer. 'And – hey, Cumulus – *where's Burnet?*'

8

Lost . . . and found

Someone is lost, and
somewhere is found.

Few things feel worse than helping search for someone who's got lost, whether it's a brother or sister at the beach, or a friend who's wandered off on a school trip. You feel sure that at any moment they'll be found, and you'll all be laughing about it; and you also feel sure you'll never, *ever* see them again. Both those things seem true at the same time, and it's awful, so you race around to try and make the feeling go away, calling their name and looking in the same places over and over again in case you somehow missed them the first time, while all the time you're searching, the ordinary world starts to seem less and less real.

That is what it was like that bleak spring dawn in a bleak, stony field beyond the motorway. As Moss and Cumulus rushed around calling for their friend and roping in any of the birds who would listen, the deer waited motionlessly, fruitlessly, for the last of the herd to appear from the direction of the distant traffic roar.

At last, Fleet volunteered to go and look at the death-route, 'In case . . .' she said, 'in case . . .' and then turned away.

The half hour Moss and Cumulus waited for her to come back was the longest of their lives. But when she returned she shook her head: 'Nothing,' she said quietly, her huge, dark eyes swimming with tears. 'I couldn't find any sign of them at all.'

'But that's good, isn't it?' said Moss. 'I mean, at least we know that they weren't . . . that they haven't been . . .'

'Only, sometimes, when one of us . . . falls – on the death-route I mean – they . . . they stop, and – and take us away,' she whispered.

'What do you mean?' cried Moss. 'Who does? Take you where?'

Cumulus spoke up slowly. 'Mortals. They eat deer just as we eat little fishes and grasshoppers. If you killed a minnow by accident, would you not take it home for the pot?'

Moss felt a great wave of faintness and nausea, and the world grew dim.

Although none of them realized it, Moss had suffered a mild concussion from being thrown around so violently on Fleet's back as she leapt across the road.

'Sit down, old thing,' came a voice. 'That's right. Head between your knees.' Cumulus's voice seemed to come from a very long way away. 'You've just had a bit of a shock. It'll pass.'

'But Cumulus,' Moss managed to whisper, 'if the worst has really happened . . . might the Mortals have taken Burnet away too? For the pot?'

Just then a familiar voice behind them cried out, 'Hello-hello!' and a hand snatched the acorn-cup hat off Moss's head.

'Why do you all look so miserable?' asked Burnet, grinning and holding Moss's cap just out of reach in an irritatingly familiar way.

A warm wave of relief washed over them. Moss burst out laughing, leapt up and hugged Burnet, shouting, 'Oh! Oh! You're alive! Burnet's alive! We're all right!'

'Well, of *course* we are,' replied Burnet. 'Whatever were you worried about?'

'But where have you been?'

'Oh, well, we had to wait an awfully long time for the chance to cross safely, that's all. You lot had all gone, and we were about to follow blindly, but then I spoke up – though I know I wasn't supposed to. "Stop!" I yelled. "Wait! We'll be killed!" And so we waited until all the death-chariots had passed – which took a long while, as you'll have noticed – and when there was a proper gap we simply walked across.'

All the deer had gathered round while Burnet was talking, including Fleet's sister, on whom Burnet had ridden. Now Fleet brought her head down low to talk to them.

'So you broke your vow to us,' she said.

Moss's heart dropped like a stone. Cumulus looked shocked, too.

'I did, ma'am,' Burnet replied staunchly. 'But I'm not sorry. It would have been madness just to follow the herd without looking or thinking.'

'For us there is safety in numbers, and security in always staying together. You Hidden Folk clearly have a more . . . individual approach to life. It was valuable on this occasion, I grant you, for it has saved the life of my sister; but a broken vow is a serious matter, and choices have consequences. We can no longer trust your word, and so we must part.'

'That's not fair!' cried Burnet.

'But, Fleet – Burnet was only trying to help,' said Moss, miserably.

Cumulus stepped forward. 'Madam, please believe us. We are heartily sorry. My friend will not utter another word, I swear it.'

But it was too late. With a last, long look from those dark eyes, Fleet turned towards the woods, and the herd turned with her. And then they simply melted away.

The three of them sat without speaking for a long time. All were exhausted, and nobody really knew what to say to Burnet, whose downcast face was streaked with tears.

At last, Cumulus spoke. 'You know, Burnet, I would have done the same thing. Honestly I would.'

'Me too,' said Moss, loyally.

'But you didn't, did you?' replied Burnet, angrily. 'It was me. I always mess up.'

'You didn't mess up – you saved a deer's life!' said Cumulus. 'Not to mention your own.'

'Why wouldn't they forgive me, then?'

'They didn't say they didn't forgive you. Only that we couldn't travel with them any more.'

'Isn't that the same thing?'

'I don't think it is, no,' replied Cumulus. 'They weren't angry. It wasn't a punishment.'

'And now we have to continue alone,' continued Burnet wretchedly, 'and I don't even know where we are!'

'Luckily you're an expert navigator,' said Moss, nudging Burnet in the ribs. 'Cheer up. I know you can get us there.'

'Of course you can,' said Cumulus. 'In fact, let's all go and have a look about, shall we? See what's what. Come on, old chum.'

'I'm still feeling a bit dizzy,' said Moss. 'Do you mind if I have a rest? You two go. I'll be right here – look, under this clump of red campion.'

'All right, then,' said Cumulus. 'Come on, Burnet. Let's go for a recce.'

'Hi! Gosh! Hello! Is it? It isn't – or is it?' came a wheezy kind of chirp.

Waking slowly, Moss looked up and saw a young bird with blue and yellow feathers bouncing on an alder twig from which dangled six yellow catkins.

'Pan's pants! Oh, pardon me,' said the bird, who was now hanging upside-down.

'Pleased to meet you,' said Moss a little hesitantly. 'Have we met?'

'I'm Zip,' chirped the bird, swinging back the right way up and fixing Moss with one bright eye. 'And you, if I'm not mistaken, are a gnome!'

'Well, *you* might say that, but *I* certainly wouldn't,' replied Moss, with a dignified expression. 'I am one of the Hidden Folk. My name is Moss, and my friends . . .'

'Moss! Well, I never,' interrupted the blue tit. 'And there's me thinking you were Cloudberry, come back at long last! Not that you lot all look the same, of course; it's just . . .'

'Quite all right,' said Moss. 'But *who* did you say you thought I was?'

'Cloudberry! You know, *Cloudberry.*' Zip was upside-down again, swinging foolishly. 'The one what went away with the Heaven Hounds. Not to worry, though; you're someone else.'

'I am. I mean, yes, I know. What are the Heaven Hounds?'

'You know: great big creatures. Always coming and going on their travels. Lots of honking.'

'Pigs?'

'Smaller.'

'Piglets?'

'Don't be daft. With *wings*.'

'Oh! You mean . . . geese?'

'Them's the ones!'

'And you're saying my cousin – you're saying that Cloudberry went away with them?'

'Oh, yes, and had a lovely foreign holiday, from what I've heard.'

'And then what?'

'And then came back, and then went off again somewhere or other. So the others all went to find out where.'

'Which others?'

'The other ones like you!'

'Do you mean Dodder and Baldmoney and Sneezewort?'

'According to my distant ancestor twice removed who went by the name of Bluebutton,' said Zip. 'And then they found Cloudberry, and they killed a giant with an oak leaf. Oh, *do* keep up.'

Moss was feeling very flustered. 'They killed a what with a what? Is that really true?'

'Search me. I don't see why not.'

'Look, Zip. All that aside: if you've heard tell of

my cousins, does that mean the Folly Brook is somewhere nearby?'

'What's the Folly Brook when it's at home?'

'A stream, with a meadow on one side and an old oak on the other; and in the oak live Dodder, Baldmoney, Sneezewort and Cloudberry! Does that ring any bells? Any bells *at all*?'

'Well, there is a stream not far off, that I do know. But we blue tits, we don't take too much notice of water; not like them kingfishers. Ooh, you've never seen the like. Bit too . . . blue, for my liking. Know what I mean? Bit *flashy*.'

'Zip,' said Moss, very slowly and clearly. 'Is my relatives' house somewhere nearby?'

'Oh, yes, absolutely. Why would you move? If you ask me, the Oak Pool is a lovely spot.'

'So – do you *know* them?'

'Me? Know? Oh, yes. Well, not personally, of course. They've been gone ever such a long time. Generations of my kind, I should think.'

'But – you said they came back!'

'That's what the story says!' wheezed the blue tit merrily. 'But then they went away again. See?'

Just then, he hopped to a higher branch, raised all the feathers on the top of his head into a sort of mohawk, and began to churr in alarm. Birds make

90

great lookouts, and most small creatures (and some big ones) take notice of them, having learnt the calls each kind of bird makes when they spot something unusual. So Moss dived into the lush green undergrowth, heart thumping, wondering what the little bird had seen: a cat, far from home and in hunting mode, looking for a snack? It was too risky to peek out through the tangled leaves and blades of grass. Far better to wait for the bird's 'all clear'.

But there was only silence. And then . . .

'Moss? Hey, Moss! Where are you?'

It was Burnet and Cumulus. Moss crawled out from under some nettles, covered in mud and tiny spiders and bits of leaf. Happily, the hair on their bodies protects Hidden Folk from most kinds of bite and sting.

'I'm here!' said Moss. 'Hello!'

'Oh! You *did* give me a fright. Why were you hiding?' asked Burnet.

'Zip the blue tit sounded the alarm, and I thought you might be a cat come to bite me on the bottom, or – or a heron about to mistake me for a newt.'

'Don't worry about bottoms or newts,' said Burnet, bouncing up and down slightly with excitement. 'Cumulus and I have some news.'

'Oh! So do I!' said Moss.'

'It's about our cousins!' continued Burnet.

'Mine is, too!'

'We've found a gnarled old oak tree with a door in the trunk, on a bend in a stream which *must* be the Folly! I saw it first, didn't I, Cumulus?'

'You did, Burnet. And—'

Then Moss and Burnet both spoke at once.

Moss said: 'They don't live there any more!'

Burnet said: 'And we think they're at home!'

OAK

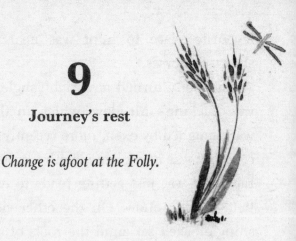

9

Journey's rest

Change is afoot at the Folly.

Bright spring sunshine sparkled on the Folly Brook, which flowed merrily amid water crowfoot and flag irises and made a wonderfully soothing sound. A drake mallard swam past, the sun flashing off his beautiful green head, followed by a swan and her fluffy grey cygnets, webbed feet paddling fast underwater while the rest of her floated by, serene. On the banks cow parsley and water forget-me-not were just coming into bloom, while a willow branch overhanging the water made a perfect perch for the pair of azure kingfishers who sometimes fished these quiet waters.

Swallows with long, forked tails swooped low over the stream, making their beeping calls. Summer visitors from Africa, they were eating the insects that gathered above the water. Their other favourite place to hunt was near animals, like sheep, or horses.

The Folly turned at a right angle. On one side was Lucking's Meadow, which in the olden days was ploughed by oxen, more recently was grazed by cows but was now planted with a crop called oilseed rape that was just getting ready to turn the whole field bright yellow. On the other side was a tiny shingle beach set amid the roots of a hollow, leafless oak, whose roots had been exposed, over very many years, by the passage of water, so that all was cavernous and dark underneath.

Hidden Folk, being very ancient themselves, love ancient, gnarled trees, and this one was no exception, for it had been home to the three friends' country cousins for a very long time. And after many years in which it hadn't been well looked after, it was now a lovely spot again – because Mortalkind had noticed that it was special, and had made a law to protect the area around the Folly, so that wild things could live safely there and not be too disturbed.

'It's *them*, I tell you!'

'But it *can't* be!'

'Well, who else would it be? A mink?'

The three Hidden Folk were crouching behind a

big clump of mallow, which was just starting to put out its pink spring flowers, Moss and Burnet arguing in that sort of cross, hissy whisper which actually travels quite far. They had crept as near as they dared to the oak to see whether their cousins really were at home.

'Look, there's no smoke coming out of the top of the hollow trunk – wouldn't they have a fire going?' asked Moss. 'I'm telling you, they've gone away.'

Moss hadn't known whether or not to believe Zip's story about Cloudberry. But now Burnet seemed so certain it was rubbish, Moss felt like defending the little bird. So, instead of finding their cousins, they were engaged in a silly game of 'who's right and who's wrong'.

'The weather's warm – they don't need to have a fire,' hissed Burnet. 'Anyway, as we told you, there was a pair of *trousers* before.'

'No trousers now. Are you sure you didn't imagine them?' snapped Moss. 'I can't even see the washing line you said they were hanging on, let alone any trousers. In fact, I'd say that is a *trouser-free zone.*'

'Oh, hush, both of you!' Cumulus hissed, and then continued, more reasonably, 'Moss, there were definitely trousers, so it can't be a mink. Minks don't, to my knowledge, favour trousers, or skirts. Now, that being the case, it rather suggests that somebody is living there who wears trousers – *our* size trousers – and has simply taken them back inside. And that's most likely to be one of our cousins, isn't it? Now we're all here, I vote we just . . . knock on the door, and find out.'

'But what if it *is* a mink?' replied Moss. 'Zip seemed very, *very* certain that Dodder and Co had gone away – for good.'

'It definitely, *definitely* won't be a mink,' Cumulus said. 'And if it is, we'll just say we got the wrong house, apologize, back away fast, and leave. But I think our cousins are in there – I really do!'

Cumulus raised an invisible hand to knock, but Burnet pointed out a little metal ball hanging to one side of the door, on a red ribbon. Rather oddly, it was the bell from a cat's collar, and, after a nod from Burnet, Cumulus gave the ribbon a tug, so that it tinkled.

There was a long wait. Moss felt rather nervous, and wondered if the others did too.

At long last there came the sound of tentative footsteps from inside. There was a shuffling sound, and then a pause.

'Er, ahem?'

The three Hidden Folk looked at one another. It definitely wasn't the nasal twang of a fitch – their word for the branch of the animal family that includes mink, weasels and stoats.

'Oi-oi,' came the voice again. 'Who is it? I'm – I mean *we* – erm – there's a lot of us here, you know, and we've all got *very pointy sticks*!'

'Good afternoon,' said Cumulus, stepping forward and addressing the still tightly closed door.

'Sticks! Big ones!' came the muffled response.

'My name is Cumulus, and these' – there was some pointless gesturing here – 'these are my friends Burnet and Moss. We're looking for Dodder, Baldmoney, Cloudberry and Sneezewort. I don't suppose you happen to know of any Hidden Folk in these parts?'

At that the door flew open, and there in front of them, holding a limp grass stalk, stood a curious little personage none of them recognized, wearing what looked a lot like a onesie made from frogskin. The frog's wizened head was still attached at the back, like a hood.

'Hidden Folk? *Hidden Folk*?! You don't mean you're – but I'm – I thought I was – oh! Well, how utterly – goodness! Come in, come in, come in!'

The three looked at one another, open-mouthed

– but the figure just turned and rushed off. There was nothing for it but to follow: Burnet first, then Cumulus and finally Moss.

The main chamber inside the oak was nothing like their home at Ash Row. There was no rush matting on the floor, and a lot more mess and disorder, with piles of rubber bands, feathers, old batteries and bottle tops, and several mysterious mechanical contraptions gathering dust. In the furthest, darkest corner was a spider web in the form of a tunnel; 'Oh, that's Hetty's quarters,' said their host, gesturing at it. 'She helps keep the mosquitoes and gnats down – she's very useful. Now, sit, sit! And tell me everything!'

Cumulus spoke up. 'Thank you, and, excuse me, but, erm – you haven't yet told us who – or what – you are.'

'Oh! I do beg your pardon. My name is Sorrel, and, despite appearances, I'm one of us – I mean, you're one of me – I mean, we're all the same!'

10

A new friend

*Three become four – and
Burnet has a shock.*

It was such a brilliant afternoon. Moss, Cumulus and Burnet sat cross-legged on the earth floor with Sorrel, and they all began to talk. The front door was propped open to let in the spring sunshine, and the Folly babbled musically as the water flowed around the corner, past the Oak Pool with its little beach in the exposed roots of the tree. At one point, Sorrel got up and fetched elderflower cordial and some delicious beechnut flapjacks saved for a special occasion, saying, 'And this *is* a special occasion, isn't it? An *extremely* special occasion,' to which they all nodded with their mouths full.

As the one who was always thinking how to turn each day's events into a story, Moss explained everything that had happened – from the morning their home was destroyed to their meeting with Mrs Ben and their encounter with Sven, including the mysterious disappearance of Cumulus's extremities, and Ro the Mortal child speaking to Moss in the Wild Argot.

'Oh, my,' interjected Sorrel at that point. 'Well, *that's* a turn-up for the books. Mortals talking, as though they're normal creatures! Imagine that!'

Then Moss told the story of their flight with the deer, and the terrifying death-route, and how they nearly lost Burnet, all the while sneaking in a few rhymes and descriptive flourishes along the way. Telling stories or reciting ballads always felt nice: it was lovely the way people listened, their faces appreciative, and it gave Moss the warm feeling that comes from knowing you're doing something well.

'And at last you arrived here!' said Sorrel at the end of the story, grinning widely. 'I must say, I'm ever so glad. This will sound silly, but I was starting to think I was the very last of the Hidden Folk – well, the last in these lands, at any rate.'

'But that's what *we* thought!' interjected Burnet. 'And Moss here had a bad dream about our kind disappearing – that's really what started us off on our adventure, just as much as losing our house, or Cumulus's see-through hands.'

'Ye-e-es, about that . . .' said Sorrel, looking

slightly uncomfortable. 'You might want to, er . . . Well, the thing is, I don't want to speak out of turn, us having just met, and I'd hate to offend, but . . .'

'What?' asked Cumulus, looking alarmed. 'Has more of me gone?'

'No, not you. It's – well, it's Burnet. I'm sorry, friend, but you might want to keep an eye on, erm, your *feet*.'

They all turned to look at Burnet – and it was immediately clear what Sorrel meant. One calloused foot had become a little bit transparent; it was still there, more or less, but you could see right through it.

Burnet leapt up in fright. 'But the deer said – they said it wasn't catching! What's going on here? Oh, what's happening? Oh, no, no *no*, come back, foot, come back – this isn't funny any more!'

'Erm, it wasn't funny when it happened to me, either!' exclaimed Cumulus.

'No, it wasn't, and it isn't,' said Moss, hoping to head off another falling-out. 'Oh, poor Burnet. Would you like a hug?'

'It seems the deer were right,' said Cumulus, 'there's something very strange going on, and perhaps it will happen to all of us, in time. We were hoping Dodder might know what to do, being the most ancient of any of us. Sorrel, do you know what's become of the four of them?'

'I'm afraid I don't. I came here after they'd gone – I lost the little brook I was guardian of a few hundred cuckoo summers ago, and wandered for a long time before I found this lovely old oak quite unoccupied, and set up home. I only know what the Stream People have told me: water vole, the King of Fishers and Eddy the otter, who lives at Rumbling Mill. As to where the rest of our kind have got to, I'm afraid I don't know. Like you, I've been worried in case I was the last of us in all the Wild World. I wouldn't like that *at all*.'

Cumulus looked grave. 'We've been saying the same. There used to be so many of us – do you remember? Every stream, ditch and wood was cared for by one or two of us; every lane or pond or corner of a field was somebody's special place. We were everywhere, once upon a time, but you're the first of our kind we've met since we left home. It's made me wonder if – well, what if the rest of us have become all invisible, like I'm beginning to?'

'Or perhaps everyone's on holiday?' said Sorrel, hopefully. 'It's perfectly possible. And anyway, there are four of us now, which is terrific, and proves us all wrong, so that's all right. Are you moving in?

Oh, say you will, I've been ever so lonely. Hetty tries her best, but spiders just aren't very talkative, you know.'

'Oh – er,' said Cumulus, glancing around at the piles of string and fragments of plastic bags and other oddments, and the general disarray and disorder. 'Well, you see, the thing is . . .'

'What Cumulus means is,' said Moss, uncomfortably. 'Well, we would, of course, and it's a very kind offer, it's just that, erm . . .'

'You've filled up the place with a load of old rubbish!' burst out Burnet. 'We couldn't possibly live here!'

There was a short silence, during which Cumulus attempted to whistle a tune and Moss felt prickly and uncomfy all over. But instead of being insulted, Sorrel simply laughed, and leant forward to pour a little more cordial into Burnet's hazelnut bowl.

'You're quite right, I have accumulated rather a lot of strange things over the years. But it's not rubbish – it's all useful, and I know exactly what's here, and where everything is. You see, I'm an inventor. I make all sorts of things!'

Dusk was falling outside and they were all starting to feel a little chilly, so they shut the front door, lit a fire and by its light went for a very quick tour of the workshop, a separate chamber at the back of the oak. Here Sorrel had created all sorts of contraptions, some of which even worked, and had thought up things that hadn't existed before. There was a rather cumbersome apparatus which used tiny fragments of broken mirror to see around corners ('excellent for spying on one's enemies', Sorrel said); a prong-like device for testing whether rhubarb is ripe, so your face doesn't go inside-out from sourness; a beetle-wheel (a bit like a tiny hamster-wheel) with a driveshaft which could be linked up with other contraptions, like the snail-shell bung-sealer or the hazelnut-cracker, if you could only persuade beetles to run on it for long enough (which nobody could). There was even the hull of a rather fine coracle which had been fitted with a small water-wheel.

Despite the fact that many of Sorrel's inventions were unfinished, and several were obviously too hare-brained to work, Moss, Burnet and Cumulus admired their new friend's cleverness very much.

That night, after they had eaten, the four of them got into their sleeping bags and lay close to the fire.

It was almost out, but the embers still glowed, sending warmth radiating out into the little room. Behind them, Sorrel's piles of Useful Things loomed dimly in the darkness; at the entrance to her silken tunnel Hetty's eight legs and eight eyes could just been seen.

'Well,' said Burnet. 'What now? We were hoping to get help from our country cousins, but it seems they've moved away.'

Sorrel was really enjoying having company and didn't want them to go. Perhaps if the trio lingered a few days, they'd realize how magical a place the Folly Brook was, and then they might want to stay for good.

'I vote you all stay with me until we've spoken to the Stream People. Perhaps one of them will have a forwarding address for your cousins, or has heard of other Hidden Folk living upstream or downstream.'

'I think that's a terrific idea,' said Moss, who wanted to unpack and tidy up a bit and perhaps live there for ever, actually, if that would be all right. Going on an adventure might be exciting, but if you're a home-loving person, it's not long until you start wanting to feel safe and indoorsy again.

'That's very kind of you, only we're in the middle of a quest, and—' said Burnet.

But Cumulus spoke over the other two. 'Thank you, Sorrel, we'd love to stay a little while. For one thing, my old bones could do with a rest. But Burnet's right: until we know why the Hidden Folk are fading, we can't settle anywhere for good.'

11

A month in the country

*Eddy the otter brings vital news
for the Hidden Folk's journey.*

Moss, Cumulus and Burnet only meant to stay a few days and nights with Sorrel on the banks of the Folly, but as it turned out they lingered long enough to see all the phases of the moon. There was a New Moon that first night, then the thinnest fingernail of the Waxing Crescent grew a few nights later into the First Quarter; a pale Waxing Gibbous that rose late one afternoon became the bright silver disc of a Full Moon that shone all night; then the Waning Gibbous shrank to Last Quarter, Waning Crescent to a fingernail moon again, and gone.

The weather was warm, with only a few gentle showers now and again to feed the new season's growth. Spring raced forward, bringing ever more fresh green leaves and bright blossom, ever more bees and butterflies and birds. The water crowfoot that streamed green in the Folly's current put out tiny white flowers like a constellation of stars, daisies and dandelions bloomed amid the thick, lush grass, bindweed coiled like miniature vines up the stems of taller weeds and unfurled pink-and-white flowers like trumpets, and oilseed rape turned Lucking's Meadow into a sheet of yellow. Every day, more butterflies tumbled and fluttered among the wild flowers, and more summer birds – chiffchaffs, whitethroats, blackcaps and willow warblers – arrived from other countries to mate, lay eggs and raise their families. Any day now the cuckoos would return to call their two-note name across the woods and valleys, telling wild creatures that another year had passed; and soon after that the swifts would scream in overhead like joyful jet fighters, catching insects high up in mid-flight.

Each day the sun set a little later in the evening, and dawn rose a little earlier. Every morning, when they woke up, they all examined their extremities, checking for further fading; but for now, the mysterious condition did not seem to be spreading or getting any worse. Secretly, Moss wondered if it was happening in age order, which meant that Sorrel might be the next one to start fading away. It seemed too serious a matter to speculate about, though.

As promised, Sorrel introduced them to the Stream People. There was Cluck the moorhen, who stalked around on enormous yellow feet; a shoal of young brown trout, which nobody could tell apart so they were all just known as Dave; an anxious water vole too shy to tell anyone her name; and Scrag the huge, hunched heron who stalked the reed beds on legs like stilts. There were rabbits, too, and rumour had it that a badger had a sett in the woods nearby. Cumulus asked around as to whether there were any hedgehogs in the area, but they had not been seen in those parts for quite some time. And every so often – not often enough – the otter family would swim past on a trip out hunting, the chattering cubs surfacing and diving like little porpoises. Sometimes they'd call in at the Oak Pool on the way back to their holt at Rumbling Mill and play a while. Everyone loves otters, and quite right too, for they are loyal, genial creatures with an excellent sense of humour, and that is one of the most important things to look for in a friend.

But while the Stream People were glad to meet them – for it had become a kind of lucky tradition to spot Hidden Folk at the Oak Pool – nobody could tell them where Dodder and Co had gone, and no one knew of any more of their kind living nearby.

One morning Moss asked to stay behind at the hollow oak for some quiet time while the others went to help Cluck build her first nest. Secretly, Moss's plan was to have a bit of a tidy-up while no one was looking. If you're a neat person, it can be very hard to live among disorder – though there's nothing more irritating to messy people than having someone 'helpfully' put away all their things. Still, a good sweep around with a broom never hurt anyone, and some of Hetty the spider's webs were very old and saggy and could be safely disposed of.

Moss carefully stripped the soft vanes from both sides of a wood pigeon's stripy tail feather, taking off the grey section and the white band to leave only the black tip, and then trimmed the shaft to a practical length (for a wood pigeon's tail feather is usually taller than any of the Hidden Folk). It made an excellent broom-cum-duster, and before long the little dwelling was looking a lot more presentable and clean.

While dusting and sweeping, Moss thought up rhymes, remembered interesting phrases and tried to come up with ways to describe all the new things that were happening – for instance, the astonishing way the King of Fishers flipped sticklebacks around so he could swallow them head-first and whole, and the way the April sunlight glittered on the Folly Brook. It was something of a habit, a way of turning everyday life into words and stories – even if the words and stories were rarely spoken aloud for fear that people might laugh, or call them pretentious or silly. If only someone could have explained that every single one of the famous writers and balladeers among the Hidden Folk had started out in just the same way.

Moss swept a pile of dust and cobwebs and frass out towards the stream so the water could carry it away (it doesn't count as litter if it's all natural materials, like bits of dead leaf – things that are already part of nature). Just then, who should appear but one of the otters. Eddy was floating downstream on his back, looking very leisurely and dapper, with his paws folded over his chest – and he had news that would bring the Hidden Folk's sojourn on the banks of the stream to an end.

'Hullo, Moss!' he cried, flipping over and

swimming, as swift and supple as an eel, to the little shingle beach, where he hauled himself out, making all the little Daves streak away in all directions to hide in the water crowfoot. With a quick shake he was nearly dry, for his fur was specially designed to keep the wet out. 'Are you doing a spot of spring cleaning?'

'That's right,' replied Moss. 'The others are all out helping Cluck build a nest – well, except for Sorrel, who's off inventing something, we think.'

'I was rather hoping I'd run into one of you,' Eddy continued, cleaning a silvery plaice scale from one whisker (he had just returned from a spot of sea fishing). 'I've some news that might interest you. Though I should warn you, it could just be the usual waterway gossip – you know how fast rumours spread up- and downstream.'

'Oh, yes,' said Moss, who didn't.

'It's like this. A black-headed gull called Esmeralda heard it from some jackdaw or other, and then she told it to a family of rabbits, one of whom told Harris the hare, who told a lamb called Number 12, apparently, who bleated it to its own reflection in the Folly and was overheard somewhere upstream by Scrag the heron, and it was Scrag who told me! D'you see?'

'Yes! I mean, no,' replied Moss. 'Which is to say, I don't think I'm quite with you. I mean, I understand the process, but . . . what actually was it that they all said?'

'Oh, *that*!' And Eddy laughed through his nose, which made a sound like a high, thin whistle. 'Well, the rumour is that there *are* other Hidden Folk left in the Wild World – though how many, I couldn't say. They make their home two hundred fields away or more, in a huge, deafening place very different to the Folly. You might have heard of it in your stories and legends: it's called the Mortals' Hive.'

When Moss told the others what Eddy had said, they didn't believe a word of it – which was hardly surprising, for the Mortals' Hive seemed like the last place in the whole Wild World you'd ever find Hidden Folk, and anyway, starlings are renowned for their tall (but often very amusing) tales. In the end, they sent word to Eddy to come back and tell them all again, leaving out no detail, and, very kindly, he agreed.

It was dusk the next day when he came, and the

birds were singing their evening chorus, which is not quite as shouty as the dawn chorus but still a lovely thing to hear. The four Hidden Folk were sitting on the shingle beach cooking minnows wrapped in wild radish leaves and set on hot stones.

When Eddy swam up they saw that Scrag the grey heron stalked behind him, all hunched and tatty-looking like a broken umbrella.

'Good evening, Scrag,' they all said, and Moss added, 'May we offer you a fish? We made extra.'

'Oh – no, thank you,' said Scrag gravely. 'I always think that cooking rather spoils them. I prefer my fish fresh, you know. *Alive*, in fact.'

'Don't mind if I do,' said Eddy, whisking a minnow from its stone and tossing it nimbly from paw to paw. 'Ow! Hot!'

They feasted, Scrag spotting an unfortunate little Dave in the shallows and swallowing him whole. Slowly the light dimmed and the birds quietened as they found roosting places for the night and one by one went to sleep. Only a lone nightingale kept on singing: he was hoping to attract a mate with his performance, and would continue his beautiful song almost all night, until dawn.

Eddy told them all what he had told Moss, Scrag nodding his long beak in agreement. 'The events currently in question unfolded just as my lutrine friend states,' he agreed, solemnly.

'Right, so the plan is to go to this Hive place and find more of our kind, and see if they're fading too and ask if they know why,' said Burnet. 'How far away did you say it was, Scrag? I'm sure I can navigate if we can think up a way to cover the distance. All I need to know is the rough direction.'

'What about the deer?' asked Moss. 'Perhaps we could get a message to them somehow, and ask their forgiveness. I really miss them, you know.'

'They'll be far away by now,' said Cumulus.

'However we travel, you do all realize I'm coming along too, don't you?' interjected Sorrel. 'You never know, I might be useful.'

Warm, flickering firelight played over the features of their ancient faces as they sat talking around the little fire. One face – the oldest – wore a worried expression.

'Let's just stop and think about this for a moment,' said Cumulus. 'It's called the Mortals' Hive for a reason: there are more Mortals there than ants in an ants' nest. I'm not sure it's safe for our kind these days.'

'But it must be, if others like us are living there,' said Sorrel.

'And anyway, how dangerous can Mortals really be?' asked Burnet, who could be reckless in pursuit of an adventure.

'What do you say to all this, Moss?' asked Eddy. 'You seem more of a stay-at-home creature, which, begging your pardon, there's nothing wrong with at all. How do you feel about this talk of going to the Mortals' Hive?'

'It's – it's so difficult,' said Moss, haltingly. 'I really like it here, by the Folly, and I love the oak tree, especially when it's tidy inside. But we have to find out what's happening to us, and where the rest of our kind are. I feel scared, if I'm honest, and part of me wants to stay here for ever. But most of me knows we have to carry on.'

12

The incredible contraption

*An exciting machine is
invented to help the four friends
on their way.*

'Now look,' said Sorrel, leading the others
along a narrow, hidden path that tunnelled
deep into the tangled green undergrowth. 'I don't
want any of you to be disappointed. It isn't quite
finished, for one thing.'

'What on earth *is* this mysterious invention?' asked
Burnet impatiently, hurrying along behind. 'Don't
think we didn't notice you sneaking off all the time!'

'My guess is that it'll be something to do with
cooking,' said Moss, who was hungry, despite the
fact that they'd only just had breakfast. 'Perhaps a
special tin box for making toast in without burning
our slices of acorn bread on the fire!'

An inquisitive pied wagtail joined the procession,
her long tail going up and down like a lever, true to
her name.

'Nope. It's definitely not a toast-contraption,' said Sorrel. 'Nearly there now. Come along.'

'I hope it's something to help my sore knee,' muttered Cumulus, who was limping a little, having slipped and fallen on the stream bank while helping Cluck find nesting materials. Only having one eye sometimes made distances and slopes hard to judge, and not being able to see your own hands can make you unsteady when you need to grab on to things.

'No, it's not something to – oh, well actually, it sort of is!' said Sorrel, stopping so suddenly that there was a minor pile-up as each of the Hidden Folk crashed into the back of the one in front and the shy wagtail flew off in alarm.

They had arrived in a little clearing in the tall, lush grass. Something very large stood there, and it was covered in an orange tarpaulin made from a plastic supermarket bag neatly hemmed with dried grass.

'Now, without further ado,' said Sorrel nervously, taking hold of one corner of the tarp in a slightly grand gesture and giving it a sudden tug. 'May I present to you ... THUNDERBOLT!'

There before them stood Sorrel's incredible contraption in all its glory: a dark red roller boot with bright yellow laces, four yellow wheels, and yellow stripes on each side.

Nobody said anything for a long moment. Sorrel looked anxiously from the red boot to the three others, and back again. The problem was, none of them had the faintest idea what it was.

'It's very . . . red,' said Moss at last.

'Oh, yes, it's extremely . . .' said Cumulus, and stopped.

'What in Pan's name *is* that thing?' blurted Burnet.

'It's *Thunderbolt*!' said Sorrel. 'I *told* you! It was once a – well, I'm not exactly sure, to be honest, because it's Mortal-made, but one of them lost it or threw it out, and I found it. But the point is not what it used to be, but what it is *now.*'

'And . . . what *is* it now?' asked Cumulus.

'This, friends, is our trusty chariot. This is how we will travel to the Mortals' Hive!'

Cumulus, Moss and Burnet looked at one another with confused expressions. Then Sorrel climbed inside the boot and was heard to fiddle around with something inside it, muttering things like, 'Just need to . . . if I can only . . . let me hook this on here . . . and then you just . . . AIEEEEEEEEEEEE!'

Suddenly, with absolutely no warning, the roller boot, with Sorrel in it, shot away into the undergrowth, incredibly fast, and disappeared.

It took the other three several minutes to find *Thunderbolt* again.

'So how do you make it *go*?' asked Moss as Sorrel climbed carefully out of the hole at the top of the roller boot and abseiled down on to the ground by the laces. 'You shot off at a fair old pace – at that rate, we could be at the Mortals' Hive in no time!'

'Yes, tell us!' said Burnet. 'Has it got a whizz-bang in it? Oh, I do hope so. I love the whizz-bangs in autumn time. They're one of the Mortals' very best inventions, don't you think?'

'No, it hasn't got a whizz-bang in it – that would be dangerous,' said Sorrel. 'And anyway, they frighten the birds.'

'What is it, then? Have you got a gang of mice in there, making the wheels go around?'

'No, no mice. Why don't you climb in and have a look!'

So Moss and Burnet clambered up the laces and disappeared into the boot while Sorrel stayed with

Cumulus in the undergrowth to explain how it worked.

'Once the basic idea had come to me it was really quite simple to make, you know. I had a pile of those brown, stretchy circles I'd been saving – did you see them, in my workshop? – and I'd already been using them to make things go, like a catapult. When you really stretch them, you see, they get terribly . . . *pingy*. They just really, really want to be *un*stretched again, and I thought I could probably use that to make some wheels go around somehow. Anyway, I did some experimenting and I came up with a system. There are four stretchy circles in there, woven together for extra pinginess, and attached to the front axle. When you wind them up with a stick and then release them, it makes the wheels go.'

'And where did you get the . . . the wheeled thing, whatever it is?' asked Cumulus.

'Oh, the chariot itself? I found it, many cuckoo summers ago. I've been waiting for a chance to do something with it!'

'Well, Sorrel. I must say, you're terribly clever. I don't know how you've done it, but I think it's quite brilliant.'

'Oh! Thank you,' said Sorrel, turning pink.

'There were some mistakes along the way. At first, I attached the . . . *pingy-power* to the back wheels, and that made the whole contraption do a backflip. With me inside!'

'Pan's teeth! I'm glad that's been ironed out. Tell me, is it difficult to steer?'

'That's the tricky bit,' admitted Sorrel. 'You see, each . . . *ping* takes you only so far, and then you have to wind up the circles again. What I've been doing is poking my head up at that point to see if *Thunderbolt* is going in the right direction, and adjusting as necessary.'

Moss's acorn-cup hat emerged from the roller boot, atop a very excited face.

'Oh, Sorrel, you *are* clever! It's so cosy in there – and safe! We could travel miles – we could even sleep in there! It would be snug, but I think we'd be warm. All we need is a cover for the entrance hole in case it rains, and I'm sure between us we can invent something for that.'

Moss clambered out, followed by Burnet.

'I think it's completely tremendous,' said Burnet. 'Let's go and have some fun, shall we? Further on, past Lucking's Meadow, there's a nice smooth path made by Mortals. We could really get up some speed!'

And so the four friends packed up the orange tarpaulin and towed *Thunderbolt* along the bank by its laces, drawing astonished stares from all the Stream People they passed. Cumulus carried the tarp, Sorrel was inside the boot, and Moss and Burnet pulled a lace each. It was quite hard going, as the spring grass was lush and thick with clover and dandelions, but at last they reached the bare earth path.

'Everybody in!' called Sorrel. Burnet went first, followed by Moss, who reached out and helped haul Cumulus in, who could be a bit creaky at times, being so incredibly old. There were some muffled exclamations from deep inside the red roller boot as everyone shuffled into place – cries of 'Ow!' and 'Get off' and 'Let me just . . .' and 'Sorry!' – and the boot itself shook slightly.

It took a few goes, but before long they could make *Thunderbolt* shoot forward without shrieking hysterically each time. They worked out how to adjust course when it slowed, and soon enough one or other of them was to be found looking nonchalantly out of the turret as the roller boot travelled, one elbow crooked over the turret's side, exactly like a soldier in a miniature tank.

'Well, what do you think? Will it do?' asked

Sorrel. It was dim in the toe of the boot, but some sunlight filtered down on Moss and Burnet, who were sitting at *Thunderbolt*'s heel end.

'Well, it's faster than us walking, that's for sure,' said Cumulus.

'It's completely, utterly and totally brilliant!' said Moss, who was feeling a bit overexcited.

'Come on, everyone!' shouted Burnet. 'No time like the present! Let's set out for the Mortals' Hive!'

13

A dip in the drink

*Not all hasty decisions turn
out to be wise ones.*

The Folly sparkled in the sunshine as it flowed past the yellow acres of Lucking's Meadow, and overhead the spring sky was blue. A tortoiseshell butterfly danced among the violets blooming on the stream bank as the birds sang cheerfully all around.

On a path beside the stream was a single, dark red roller boot with two yellow stripes. A tiny face appeared at the opening, disappeared again – and all of a sudden the boot whizzed off as if by magic, a cry of triumph issuing from within. Further down the path it rolled slowly to a halt. There came a pause, and some muttering – then off it flew again.

'Thataway!' called Burnet, whose head kept popping up to check on their direction.

'Faster, faster!' cried Moss each time Sorrel wound up the rubber bands that powered the wheels.

'Did I remember to lock the front door?' muttered Sorrel, not really expecting an answer from anyone.

Meanwhile, Cumulus, deep in the toe of the boot, was quietly thinking about sudden decisions, which were sometimes brave and sometimes foolish, and how it can be hard to tell which it is until you know how things turn out. It's definitely true that sometimes you have to just do a scary thing quickly, without worrying too much, or you never will; but at other times it's better to plan and prepare – and Cumulus was thinking that maybe going to the Mortals' Hive in a home-made chariot might be the second sort of situation, when the boot slammed into a large clump of dock at high speed. There was a jolt, the feeling of briefly being airborne, and then, with a splash, *Thunderbolt* began filling up with water and sinking to the bottom of what could only be the Folly Brook.

Moss bobbed up to the surface, doggy-paddled to the bank and looked back. There in mid-stream was Burnet, hanging on to the submerged *Thunderbolt* by one of its laces, then taking a big breath of air and bravely going back under to haul Cumulus out of the boot and over to the bank. But where was Sorrel?

'Oi! Hey! Gerroff!' came a familiar voice. And there, swimming with his head well above the stream, was Eddy, and in Eddy's mouth was Sorrel, held carefully in his sharp teeth but struggling and protesting all the same.

'What did I tell you?' said Eddy after he had spat Sorrel on to the stream bank with the others.

'You said I should learn to swim,' said Sorrel, 'but, as I've told you before, I have absolutely no intention of getting into the Folly on purpose, so why would I?'

'Because you live beside water, and accidents happen,' said Eddy. 'Like this one. Good thing for you I was passing – and it's just as well I didn't take you for a frog, given that ridiculous outfit. I could have eaten you whole!'

'Excuse me, but it's very rude to pass comment on another creature's attire,' said Sorrel, standing up as tall and dignified as was possible, water dripping a bit slimily from the frogskin onesie.

Eddy turned to the rest of them. 'Did you all take a dip in the drink? Everyone all right?'

'Oh, we're all right,' said Cumulus. '*We* can all swim, you see, even Moss. We were never in danger of being washed downstream.'

'In fact, I can swim so well I was able to rescue Cumulus!' boasted Burnet.

'I was absolutely fine,' replied Cumulus. 'I would have floated out quite easily, given time.'

'Before you go, Eddy,' said Sorrel, in a wheedling voice, 'I don't suppose you'd be able to rescue my – *our* chariot – and tow it back to the Oak Pool? We'd all be terribly grateful.'

'Especially you?' asked Eddy. 'After all, I *did* save you from washing away.'

'Especially me.' Sorrel grinned. 'Thank you, Eddy. I'm sorry I squirmed.'

Six o'clock the next morning, and in one of the topmost twigs of a hollow oak whose roots were exposed by the Folly rushing around a bend sat Spangle the starling. His black eyes were bright and mischievous, his beak was open, and from it came some of the most extraordinary sounds you've ever heard: there were cheeps that sounded like a squeaky dog toy, clicks and whirrs, robotic beeps, and whistles like a happy builder on a building site. The short feathers of his throat moved as he poured forth this unusual performance, showing just how hard he was working at it.

At last he gave a cackle, shook out his feathers,

and dropped easily down to the bank of the stream, accompanying himself with the descending sound of a trombone. 'That should wake 'em, I reckon,' he said as he fluttered to a halt outside the neat little door and folded his wings away. And sure enough, the door creaked open and Sorrel's bleary face peeped out.

'Morning, Boss,' said Spangle, 'what sort of time d'you call this? The sun's been up for hours, you know. The message I got said to come first thing!'

'Morning, Spangle,' yawned Sorrel. 'We're ever so sorry – we stayed up late last night, drying our clothes by the fire due to yesterday's, er, unexpected watercourse incursion. We'll be right with you.' And the door closed again.

'For Pan's sake, some people,' muttered Spangle to himself.

Before long the Hidden Folk had roused themselves from sleep and were gathered, squinting in the sunshine, on the little shingle beach. Moss had quickly made some acorn fritters and handed them around along with a little pot of honey for everyone to munch on.

'Now, firstly, thank you for coming, Spangle,' began Cumulus. 'It's lovely to see you again, and it's ever so kind of you to help.'

'Nothing long,' replied the smart bird, eyeing the fritters a little beadily. 'What can I do you for?'

'It's like this. We want to travel to the Mortals' Hive – '

'Oh, is it?'

'Is what?'

'You lot, going to the Mortals' Hive. Never mind, Boss. You carry on.'

'As I was saying,' continued Cumulus, 'we want to go to the Mortals' Hive, and we have a contraption – a fine one, I might add, if a little damp – to take us there. We've asked you to come today because we need your advice about the route.'

'Advice, right, gotcha. First things first, though: can I have one of them?'

'Oh – of course,' said Moss, stepping forward. 'I do apologize, I should have offered. I don't know what's become of my manners today, I really don't. Honey?'

'No, ta, it jams up me beak. Now, where were we? Oh, yeah, the Mortals' Hive. It's upstream, over *that*away.' And he indicated the direction with a flick of his sleek little head. 'Two days' flight for me, stopping off for snacks and the odd nap. A quicker bird could do it in a day, if the weather held – remind me about that, 'cos we need to discuss.

First you have to go up over a high moor, you get me? Not much to look at, just brown hills covered in heather and gorse, big grey stones with bracken around 'em, and sheep. Look out for the ravens – now *there's* a bird! Anyway, after a bit you'll see it in the distance like a big grey wart, or if it's night, lit up orange. There's more and more roads and railway lines and houses and whatnot as you get closer, busier and busier down below. Then, before you know it, you're right over it. Oh my days! So noisy and exciting. And then down you go into the smells and the warmness and the honking and the swarms of Mortals and you find somewhere to land. Like a tree, if there is one. Or one o' them sticky-up metal things on a roof.'

Burnet had been listening very carefully, nodding thoughtfully at the mention of the weather. 'The moor you mentioned – is there a road that crosses it? A smooth one, without any big clumps of dock, or any other plant, for that matter?'

'Yes, Boss,' said Spangle. 'We birds often use it to help navigate, as it goes. It's a thin, wiggly one – not too many of them death-chariots on it, I shouldn't think.'

'That's good. Do you think we could travel along it safely?'

Spangle looked doubtful. 'P'raps . . . if you were walking at night time, I suppose. But it'd take you for ever.'

Sorrel stepped forward. 'Ah, but you see . . . our contraption will help us travel at speed, as long as the surface is smooth. Please, come and see!'

Spangle looked a little sceptical, but Sorrel led him off into the undergrowth where the still-damp *Thunderbolt* was hidden, Cumulus, Moss and Burnet following along behind.

Proudly, Sorrel parted the tall grass to show Spangle their creation. In response, the bird gave a low whistle, and then walked all the way around it, eyeing it carefully and emitting a series of soft clicks as its inventor excitedly explained how it was powered.

'What it is . . .' Spangle said at last. 'What it is, right . . . I mean, I gotta say, this is *something*. I mean, it's a *lot*. Only . . .'

'What?' asked Sorrel.

'I gotta be straight with you, Boss. It ain't gonna work, and I'll tell you for why. You see, almost the whole of the first bit is *uphill*.'

14

A change of plan

*Spangle dashes Sorrel's hopes
– but all is not lost for the
next stage of the quest.*

'A friendly duck?'

'They're . . . not the brightest.'

'Blackbirds?'

'Not big enough.'

'A . . . swan, then?'

'Too stuck-up – it'd never agree.'

'Well, what about you, can't you take us?' Burnet asked Spangle, exasperated. 'Starlings are friendly *and* clever, isn't that right?'

The four Hidden Folk were sitting with Spangle in the lowest crook of the hollow oak's leafless branches. Sorrel looked crestfallen; it had been a blow to discover that *Thunderbolt* wasn't going to be able to take them on the next stage of their journey. Burnet, though, was extremely excited: since hearing that their cousin Cloudberry had gone on migration with the Heaven Hounds – the geese – dreams of finding a way to get up in the sky and fly with the birds had filled every waking hour. Now Spangle had promised to try and find a feathered friend who would give them a lift for at least part of the way; all that remained was to decide which kind of bird would be the best flying taxi service for them all.

'Truesay,' replied Spangle. 'Friendly *and* clever is right. But if a blackbird's too small to carry one of you lot far, how d'you think a starling's gonna do it? Plus, we're proper *flappy* when we're flying. You'd turn green in five seconds, Boss.'

'Aren't you curious to know why we want to go to the Hive in the first place, Spangle?' Moss asked, watching a bright green caterpillar laboriously inching its way up a nearby twig.

'Way I see it, that's your business,' replied the starling. 'Me, I don't make a habit of noseying about. There's not much in the Wild World I'd be surprised by, anyway. Know my motto? Live and let live.' And with that he leant forward, opened his beak and snapped up the caterpillar, swallowing it whole.

'All right, what about a buzzard?' Cumulus suggested. 'They're definitely big enough.'

'Won't go into the Hive. They might be hench, but they ain't brave.'

'Jackdaw?'

'Don't trust 'em. Funny eyes.'

'A puffin?'

'Now you're just being silly.'

'Ooh, I know! An owl!' cried Moss. 'Two owls! The Bens!'

'You lot are mates with *actual wols*?' asked Spangle. 'Oh my days.'

'Owls. Not wols.'

'Whatever. They're spooky, you get me? Not to mention, they're always throwing up. Ooh, no, ta.' And he roused his feathers so that they all stuck out, shivered, then stood up tall and shook out his short tail.

'Look, Spangle,' interrupted Cumulus, in a reasonable tone of voice. 'You've said no to every bird we've suggested. Who do *you* think should take us to the Mortals' Hive?'

'Well, it's obvious, innit? You want a proper good flier, and you want a city bird, one with a bit of nous – not one of your country lot who'll fall out of the sky with fright the first time they hear a *wee-woo*, you get me?' Here, bobbing his head up and down, he gave a highly accurate impression of a siren.

'What you want, my friends, is a pigeon,' he continued. 'Not the big, fat ones from these ends, what sit around in trees looking idle and going *coo*.

No, their cousins: same but different. I'm talking about a proper Hive pigeon – what you might also call a rock dove, as was.'

'Oh, no, we don't,' said Burnet, who by now was bouncing up and down on the twig with excitement.

'Don't what?' asked Spangle.

'Want one,' replied Burnet.

'Don't we?' asked Moss, Cumulus and Sorrel, in unison.

'No – we want *four*!' Burnet replied.

Spangle's idea was a good one. Urban pigeons are some of the very best fliers in the avian kingdom, breathtakingly fast and able to twist and turn and perform feats of aerial derring-do; they're also incredible navigators who can find their way across vast distances using an inbuilt compass so good we humans haven't yet fully understood how they do it. And they're brave and clever and can put up with injured feet, human litter and mess and most kinds of pollution. In short, they're perfectly cut out for life in the big city. Just as the little starling had said, they have 'nous'.

As soon as it had all been agreed, Spangle flew off to round up some volunteers, promising to return with them the next morning, ready to set out. 'Bound to be a few of 'em commuting in – no skin off their beaks to take a passenger,' he said.

'Tomorrow morning? So soon?' Moss asked. Cumulus looked up, also a little concerned.

'Remember, I said before, about the weather?' Spangle replied. 'There's a storm coming in, as Burnet here will testify. You want to get well ahead of that, if you ask me.'

The four Hidden Folk spent the rest of the day each packing a backpack with their belongings and getting ready to leave the Folly Brook behind. Then they bade farewell to the King of Fishers, who wished them good luck before shooting off upstream to look for Eddy and let him know that they were leaving. They waved to all the little Daves who swam in formation under the water, blowing bubbles and waving their fins, and said goodbye to Zip the blue tit, who swung upside-down from a hazel twig and replied with a chirp. Most of the other birds were too busy to stop and chat, it being springtime: hidden everywhere in the thickets, woods and undergrowth near the stream were nests filled with broods of hungry, gaping chicks demanding to be fed. It felt sad to leave the Folly without seeing the young birds fledge.

At dusk, Eddy and his partner Fleek swam up against the current, where the water was deepest, their low heads barely breaking the surface of the stream. Then they hauled themselves out and shook themselves, bright droplets spraying from their fur, and whistled softly for the Hidden Folk. They all had an excellent evening on the stream bank, telling stories, playing games and eating freshwater mussels that Fleek dived for, cracking open the shells with her strong white teeth. It wasn't a sad occasion, because otters are very cheerful animals; and as they had never been to the Mortals' Hive and had no wish to go, they couldn't quite believe in it, or its dangers. More practical than imaginative, at the end of the evening the pair simply slipped away into the water with a light-hearted, 'Cheerio!'

It was colder and breezier the next morning when Moss, Cumulus, Burnet and Sorrel found themselves sitting cross-legged for one last time around the campfire which burnt in a circle of pebbles on the shingle beach. Eight stickleback fillets threaded on hazel twigs were hanging above the fire to smoke, while in the ashes around it four loaves of conker bread were baking, each one inside a scrubbed-out mussel shell.

'D'you know, I've wanted to fly ever since I can remember,' said Burnet happily. 'I can't for the life of me think why I've never arranged it before. As soon as I heard about Cloudberry and the Heaven Hounds, I said to myself, "Pan's teeth! Whyever didn't I think of that?"'

'It's an excellent idea,' said Sorrel. 'Good old Spangle. I can't wait to get up there and study how their wings work – have I told you all that I want to make a flying machine one day?'

'Aren't you feeling sad about *Thunderbolt*?' asked Moss.

'Oh, no, I've quite got over that. The important thing about being an inventor is that you learn from everything that happens: it's not failure, it's just new information for next time. You can't go around taking things personally, or every setback would make you want to give up.'

'I think that's an excellent way of looking at it,' said Cumulus.

'And, anyway,' said Sorrel, 'who's to say that *Thunderbolt* won't be perfect for some other adventure, when we get back from the Mortals' Hive?'

'Pan willing,' said Moss, quietly.

Cumulus took Moss's hand in two invisible ones and squeezed. 'Are you worried, Moss?'

'A little bit,' Moss replied. 'It's just . . . well, Spangle said – and Burnet agreed – that there's bad weather coming. It feels a little bit frightening to think that we could be up in the sky, on a bird's back, in a storm.'

The others nodded soberly. It *was* frightening, and so was the place at the end of their journey – something none of them had really mentioned yet. Perhaps now was a good time to talk everything through, Moss thought. They had been so focused on getting airborne that they had almost forgotten the reason for it: their need to find out the fate of the other Hidden Folk, and how it tied in with the fading away of Cumulus and Burnet. For Moss had seen Cumulus having a wash in the Oak Pool, and knew something Sorrel and Burnet didn't: the process of disappearing hadn't halted, and, despite having promised to tell the others everything, under that robe Cumulus's arms and legs were now see-through.

'Look, everyone. There's something I think we should talk about, something a bit . . .' Moss began – but suddenly, with a loud beating of wings and a great rush of air that sent the smoke from the campfire billowing, the pigeons arrived.

15
Flight

*The adventurers slip the bonds
of earth, chased by a storm.*

'What, *now*? Really? *Really*, everyone? Just like that, we . . . fly away? I mean, Spangle's not even with you, so you four birds could be anyone, frankly, and the fact is, we haven't even been – I mean, I'm Moss, hi, hello, very pleased to meet you, and you're . . . well, pigeons, clearly, but I'm sorry, how about you start by telling me your *names?*'

Moss was extremely nervous about flying up into the sky on the back of a bird, and was squashing that fear by being cross, which is a far easier feeling to feel – though a little unpleasant for everyone else. Fortunately, Cumulus and Burnet had been friends with Moss for several centuries and knew exactly what was going on.

'Er – greetings, friends,' Burnet said to the four pigeons, stepping forward and laying a calming

143

hand on Moss's back.

Each of the pigeons had a different plumage pattern: one was pale grey with a purple-and-green neck, one was warm brown with a cream rump and tail, one had smart black bars on its wing tips, and the last one was dark, with speckled wings and a golden eye.

'We will be eternally in your debt for your gracious offer of assistance in attaining the Mortals' Hive,' Burnet continued, trying to smooth over Moss's accidental rudeness. 'Spangle the starling has informed us that you are peerless fliers, supreme among all the avifauna that occupy these lands, and that you carry great wisdom within you, pertaining to the—'

'Pan's pants – what's it on about?' muttered one of the pigeons to another, out of the side of its beak.

'Search me,' the other one replied. 'I think it said hello, but after that I sort of . . . zoned out. Are they elves?'

'Funny little creatures, whatever they are. One's got no feet, and one's got no hands – have you seen?'

Just then, Spangle landed in a great explosion of clicks and beeping sounds, some of which sounded suspiciously like swear words.

'Oh my *days*,' he said, when he'd settled his

feathers. 'Sorry I'm late, I roosted in a garage last night and I had to wait for the Mortals to come and open the doors. I always forget how late they sleep. Right, introductions, 'cos I know you pigeons want to get going. This is Cumulus with the long hair and no hands, Moss in the acorn-cup hat, Burnet with the skirt and no feets, and Sorrel in the frogskin onesie' – he nodded at each of them with his beak – 'and on the bird side we've got Rani there with the go-faster stripes, Reni in cream and brown, Ron with the flashy neck, and over there is Roger. You get me? Right, then. See ya later!'

'Wait!' cried Moss.

'Oh, what *now*?' sighed the pigeon called Rani, giving her beautiful barred wing feathers a quick preen.

'It's just that – I was wondering, shouldn't we have a . . . a flight plan? And is there anything we need to know about the journey, or what it'll be like when we get there?'

'Know what, you're quite right, Boss,' said Spangle. 'Quite right. Moss is *quite right*!' he repeated, addressing the four pigeons. 'I've been so rushed off my wings I hardly know where my beak's at. All right, team briefing. Gather round, gather round. Pigeons: like I said last night, these four are wanting a lift to the Hive – the closer to the centre you can get 'em the better. Now remember, they've never been there before, so think about where you're going to drop them off. Pick somewhere they can pitch their tents safely for the night – one of them really big parks, maybe, the kind with messy bits, not the really neat ones. But don't go joining a flock of your lot eating bread off the ground, you get me? You know who throws the bread down? *Mortals.* And, unlike you four, *this* lot don't want to be seen by *them* lot. You get me?'

'Got you,' said Ron.

'Roger that,' said Rani.

'What's that now?' asked Roger, cocking his golden eye.

'Not you,' hissed Reni.

'Ahem! Hidden Folk!' continued Spangle. 'Pay attention: when you first climb on to the back of your pigeon, make sure your backpack is settled on your shoulders securely, and then find and hold the quill of a feather in each hand – the quill is the hard bit in the middle, all right? Don't go pulling out handfuls of their underdown – it's bad manners. Do *not* grab at their wings, and try not to shriek – it's very off-putting – even if they bank, dive, twist or roll, which they might, depending on hazards.

146

Lean *into* any corners, not out, or you'll make 'em unstable, and that, believe me, is something you do not want. Mostly, just . . . sit tight and be sensible, all right? Oh, and try to enjoy it. You're about to do what every earthbound animal in the whole Wild World dreams of: you're gonna fly!'

As he spoke, the four pigeons lowered themselves into a crouch so that the Hidden Folk could climb aboard. Moss was closest to the dark-feathered, golden-eyed bird called Roger, and although it felt very strange to be touching a bird's feathers, Roger didn't seem to mind it at all.

'Are you sitting comfortably, little friend?' he asked kindly. 'Found a couple of good strong feathers to hold on to?'

'Yes, thanks,' replied Moss in a slightly shaky voice. 'Do tell me if I'm doing anything wrong.'

'Oh, I will, don't you worry about that. But you'll be fine, I promise. There'll be a bit of flapping during take-off, so grip with your knees. After that, it's just you, me, and the endless freedom of the skies.'

'And the others!' said Moss. 'Don't forget about them, or leave them behind!'

'I won't, I promise. Now, are you ready?'

Moss took a deep breath and swallowed hard. 'As I'll ever be, I suppose.'

'That's the spirit. And we're off!' With that, Roger spread his wings and, with Moss on his back, whose eyes were squeezed shut, he simply jumped into the waiting air.

For a few moments it seemed to Moss that all was confusion: the bird's strong wings beating so close, a tummy-dropping lifting feeling like being on a rollercoaster, a great rushing of air all around. But then Roger's wings settled into a steady rise-and-fall pattern and things seemed to level out. Curiosity overcame fear, and Moss decided to take a peek.

And instantly it was wonderful. Below them – far below – was the patchwork green of the countryside: fields and hedges, the darker shapes of woods, and the bright line of the Folly Brook catching the light. The sun was warm on their backs, and above and around them there stretched the vast blue arena of the sky. Moss couldn't help grinning, and let out an excited shout: 'Woo-hoo!'

'WA-HEY!' came an answering cry, as beside them the pigeon named Rani appeared, carrying a laughing Burnet on her back.

'Isn't it amazing?' shouted Burnet.

'It's *so* amazing!' replied Moss. 'Where are the others?'

'Look behind you!'

Holding on carefully, Moss turned – and there were Reni and Ron, wings beating steadily, eyes focused forward, their passengers smiling in delight – even Cumulus, whose green hat had immediately blown off and been lost. Sorrel even let go with one hand to give the leading pair a quick wave. Moss, heart soaring like the birds that were bearing them, felt any remaining nervousness melt away.

They were gaining height, and the world below was becoming smaller and smaller. And, somehow, it felt as though all of their worries were also getting smaller – as though they barely mattered at all. Flying though the sky, far above everything down on the ground, was like entering an entirely new world.

'Oh – but we didn't say goodbye to Spangle!' Moss exclaimed after a while.

'Don't you worry about him,' said Roger. 'He said he'd follow along at some point. You'll see that one again!'

Moss gazed around and tried to take it all in, but it still felt overwhelming. 'We could fly anywhere – anywhere at all!'

'That's right, little friend. Isn't it wonderful? You can see why Mortals are always trying to copy us. Since the dawn of time they've envied us our wings.'

'So have I!' Burnet shouted over, from Rani's back.

'And me!' came Sorrel's voice from behind. 'I've been studying how Rani does it – it's more complicated than I'd thought.'

'Oh, yes, it's not just a case of going *flap-flap-flap-flap*,' Rani said, tipping sideways into a graceful banking roll. Burnet let out an excited shriek.

Moss settled into it. Ahead lay the horizon, where the blue of the sky met the misty greys and browns of the moorland they were flying over. Far, far below snaked a tiny line with tiny glinting shapes upon it: not the Folly, but a road across the moor, dotted with cars.

Just imagine: in each of those cars there were people – grown-ups driving, perhaps with kids in the back, talking or listening to music or staring out of the window; and none of them the least bit aware that high, high above them flew four urban pigeons, each with one of the Hidden Folk on its back, all of whom would get to the big city long before them. What an extraordinary thing.

'How are you doing?' Roger asked after a while. Moss had to lean forward to catch his words before the breeze snatched them away. 'Would you like me to perform some aerial stunts for you, like Rani did for Burnet?'

'No, thank you,' said Moss. 'Although I am enjoying it – much more than I'd expected to!'

'You looked ever so worried to begin with!'

'I – I didn't want to fly, to be honest. I'm not as brave as my friends.'

'Oh, I think you're braver! It's easy to do something you're not frightened of. To me, bravery is about feeling a bit scared, and doing it anyway. Which is exactly what you did.'

Moss's nut-brown face, from chin right up to acorn-cup hat, blushed with pleasure. 'Well, thank you very much. I don't even know what I was worried about now – it seems quite silly of me.'

'Not at all,' replied the bird. 'Going from one element to another – whether it's earth to water or up into the air – should always be taken seriously. And anyway, you were quite correct to be concerned about the weather. Look over there!'

Moss peered into the distance. A huge cloud with a wide, spreading top seemed to tower into the sky.

'See that? That's a storm cloud,' said Roger, 'and it's no laughing matter – there's high winds, freezing air and hailstones flying about in there, not to mention thunder and lightning. But don't worry, we set out early enough. We'll beat the weather!'

On they flew, onwards, as the skies clouded over,

until the sun no longer shone warmly on their backs. Slowly the greys and browns of the open moorland below them gave way to the green squares of fields, and then there began to be more buildings dotted among the woods and pastures until, looking down, Moss realized that they were flying over roofs and busy roads.

'Is this it? Is this the Mortals' Hive?'

'Oh, gosh, no,' replied Roger. 'It's far, far bigger than that.'

And, sure enough, the streets and houses gave way to green again, and they were once more over countryside. They descended a little and flew lower than they had over the moorland, though still high above the tallest treetops. They saw winding country lanes that snaked between bushy hedges; they glided and banked over the silvery disc of a lake; they passed over the flat grey roofs of a massive warehouse with hundreds of lorries parked outside. And all the time the light was slowly fading from the sky as the clouds thickened and gathered, as though a dimmer switch was gradually being turned down on the day.

At last, they flew over a wide, busy motorway, after which there were more and more buildings below. Moss's eye was caught by a movement: a long train raced in the same direction as they were going, on rails that glinted dully under the grey sky. Now there was only the occasional green of a park or a sports pitch; mostly, what they were flying over was a network of streets and terraced houses stretching out into the distance – far, far bigger than any Mortal-made place they had seen before. The air was full of the roar of distant traffic, and it smelt different. The ride was also becoming less smooth, and Moss was having to hold on quite tight; it wasn't that Roger wasn't flying so evenly, it was that an easterly wind had got up, and was starting to buffet them about.

'This is the Hive!' came a shout.

Moss, crouching low on Roger's back, looked over at Cumulus, white hair now streaming backwards and pointing down with an empty sleeve past Ron's toiling wings – and it was at that very moment that the first huge raindrops hit.

'Hold hard!' cried Roger, and Moss gripped tightly with knees and hands. 'I'm taking you down earlier than planned!'

He banked sharply to the left and went into a steep downward glide, the other three pigeons not far behind. The streets, roofs and chimneys grew bigger and bigger, the air now teeming with raindrops, which soaked Moss to the skin.

'INCOMING!' shouted Roger as he zoomed down out of the sky above a busy city street full of cars. Moss squeezed both eyes tightly shut.

'Roger that!' came three shouts from behind him.

'Who, me?' replied Roger, glancing behind and nearly falling out of the sky.

'Oh, never mind!' came the faint reply.

Roger swooped into a dark road tunnel, out the other side, under the lowest branches of a tree that grew by the roadside and up to a messy old magpie's nest, sheltered by leaves. With much fluttering of wings, he landed, and within seconds Ron, Rani and Reni were beside him.

As the rain poured down all around, drenching the cars and shops and houses, the four Hidden Folk looked at one another, eyes wide.

'W-w-we made it, then,' Moss managed at last.

'We absolutely did,' said Burnet. 'I knew we would!'

'May Pan protect us,' said Cumulus softly, whose white hair stood out in all directions. 'For we have arrived in the Mortals' Hive.'

THORN

16

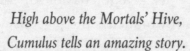

In the belly of the beast

High above the Mortals' Hive,
Cumulus tells an amazing story.

It was a rainy Tuesday teatime towards the end of May, and in an old nest in a tall street tree near the heart of a big city sat four bedraggled Hidden Folk and the four tired pigeons who had flown them all the way there from the lush green country-side. It was a plane tree, and on its trunk the bark flaked off in patches; this was the tree's clever way of coping with the pollution given off by the slow-moving traffic that crawled past. The pollution was also trapped by tiny hairs on the tree's leaves and then washed away whenever it rained. All in all, the plane tree did an excellent job of cleaning the city air, as well as providing somewhere for birds and squirrels and thousands of creatures to live.

'It smells different here,' remarked Sorrel, sniffing the air. Like animals, Hidden Folk have very sensitive noses and can smell a great many more things than Mortals can.

'I was just thinking that,' replied Burnet. 'It's unusual, isn't it? Perhaps we'll stop noticing it after a while.'

'You will – just give it a day or so,' said Cumulus.

In the nearby branches the pigeons were shaking the rain from their feathers and giving themselves a quick preen; they were quite used to traffic and noise, and felt very much at home. Rani had even drawn her nictitating membrane across her eyes (this is an extra eyelid that birds and reptiles have, that goes side to side). She was attempting a quick nap, which was fair enough: while the plane tree kept the worst of the weather off them, the rain was still hammering down and there was nothing for it but to wait it out.

'Tell you what, I've never seen so many death-chariots,' said Moss, worriedly. 'I'm glad we're up here and not down there!'

'At least they're all going slowly – not like the ones on the big road we crossed with the deer,' Burnet replied.

'Here in the Mortals' Hive they tend to come out twice a day – a few hours after sunrise, and then again as the sun begins to sink towards the horizon,' said Roger. 'In between, it gets a little quieter. I don't know why.'

'Maybe it's like rabbits,' said Moss. 'You know how they come out twice a day to feed, at sunrise and sunset – when the dew is on the grass? Perhaps it's like that, and the death-chariots have two feeding times.'

'Yes, that could be it,' nodded Burnet.

'Speaking of food, does anyone fancy a snack?' asked Moss. 'I'm starving.'

'Me too!' piped up Sorrel. 'I could murder a mushroom.'

'I'd make *extremely* short work of a nice, juicy blackberry,' said Moss.

'I'm the hungriest,' said Burnet. 'I could polish off a whole Dave!'

Unfortunately they didn't have any of those delicious things, but Moss passed around some conker-skin biltong and they chewed on that, dangling their tiny legs over the cars and buses and motorbikes passing below. They looked down and saw a couple of patches of pavement spattered with white droppings. These were directly below the best branches for birds to perch on.

Before long the rain began to ease and the sun peeked out from the clouds, making the wet pavements shine and reflecting off the windscreens of the traffic. Rani woke up and shook out her feathers, and Roger fluttered over to the Hidden Folk for a chat.

'So here's the thing,' he began. 'We promised Spangle we'd take you to a park where you could pitch your tents, but, as you know, the weather's forced us down early. We're happy for you to saddle up again and we can fly a bit further in and drop you off – there's a couple of big grassy areas I know of, and Reni and Ron know of some little green corners, too. But I was thinking – the grass down there is going to be ever so wet after all this rain. Do you really want to camp out tonight?'

'What's the alternative?' asked Moss.

'Well, this nest's not the worst place in the world, you know. And when the lights come on the views will be tremendous. Just throwing it out there as an option.'

The four friends looked at one another. It wasn't what they had envisaged for their first night in the Mortals' Hive, but, truth be told, they all had bruised bums from riding their pigeons – Burnet, who wore a kilt, especially – and none of them really wanted to fly much further.

'I say we stay here,' said Moss.

'Me too,' said Sorrel.

'Me three,' said Burnet, taking the 'Stanley' knife and trimming back some of the pokiest twigs so that the bowl of the nest became an almost-comfortable place to rest.

It was early evening now, and lights were starting to come on all over the Hive. The brake lights and headlamps of cars made ribbons of red and white, while the windows of the terraced houses glowed golden. Here and there were tall tower blocks, each one twinkling with dozens of bright squares. The city stretched out all around them as intricate and full of wonders as a beehive, or a termite mound, or a living coral reef.

'Wow-ee,' whispered Sorrel. 'I didn't expect it to be so beautiful!'

'Nor me,' said Burnet.

'I thought it would be ugly and horrible, with no trees or living things – but it isn't like that at all!' said Moss. 'How about you, Cumulus?'

'Oh,' said their old friend, 'I knew that already. You see, I've been here before – many years ago.'

Moss and Burnet looked at one other, open-mouthed with surprise.

'How come? Is it an adventure story? Tell us! Oh, please tell us!' said Burnet.

'Only if you want to, though,' added Moss, who had noticed that their old friend's eyes looked sad.

'It was – it was like this,' Cumulus began, a little haltingly. 'As you know, before I came to live with you two in the ash tree, I had been wandering the Wild World for a long while.'

Moss and Burnet nodded. They still remembered as though it was yesterday the day they'd met Cumulus, who was even more impossibly ancient than they were – as well as being, at that time, tired and thin and quiet. As was polite, their new friend told them a little of what had happened, but as the decades passed and they saw and did so many things together, it didn't seem important to find out what had gone on before they all met – especially given that Cumulus never, *ever* brought it up.

'After I lost my beloved pond, I set out to try and understand the great change that was happening – the greatest change, it seemed to me, since Mortals had first appeared in the Wild World.'

'What kind of change?' asked Moss.

'Well, for a long time they had lived by gathering wild foods and hunting and fishing, just like we do. Then they learnt to plough the land and grow crops, and they settled down instead of moving around, and slowly, very slowly, they altered some of Pan's creatures to make unwild animals that were more useful to them, like cows, and pigs, and sheep.'

'And dogs and cats,' interjected Burnet.

'And dogs and cats, yes. But that wasn't the great change I mentioned. During this time their numbers increased, but only slowly, and they lived in settlements scattered all over the land, some small and some a little bigger, but nothing like the hives most live in now. Back then, we lived with them and among them, and they knew of us, if only dimly – like a story you've half-forgotten, or an image from a dream.

'And then, more than two hundred cuckoo summers ago, something happened in the world of Mortals. It was like . . . a great acceleration. Suddenly, or so it seemed, they had all sorts of interesting contraptions they had never had before, and it was so exciting to watch! Sorrel, I'm sure you remember it. But in some places the air filled with smoke, and many of the rivers began to die.

'And I noticed another thing then, although it's hard to describe. It was as though . . . as though they forgot that they were part of the Wild World, and that they needed the bees and the animals and the trees and everything else. That frightened me, and so I set out to try to understand what was happening. And in my wanderings I came here, to the Mortals' Hive.'

'What was it like?' asked Moss.

'Well, there were no death-chariots then, of course, but they were busy building their edifices, and it was loud and smelt of smoke and horse dung and Mortalkind, and it was beautiful and terrifying and intoxicating, and despite myself I loved it very much.

'But I saw that as the Mortals expanded their Hive, they covered over the places that had existed beforehand – the fields and orchards, the little copses and thickets, the ponds and heaths and streams. And the Hidden Folk who had for so long looked after those places had to try and find some-where else to live, as did the nightingales and the dormice and the lizards and so on. And as more Mortals streamed in to live here, the Hive kept on expanding to fit them all in.'

'Gosh,' said Sorrel, 'do you mean to say that deep under all these streets and buildings are hills and valleys?'

'And rivers, too!' replied Cumulus. 'Mortals sent most of them underground so they wouldn't be in the way, and now they see no sunlight, and have no guardians at all.'

'So . . . what happened to all the Hidden Folk

who lived here before the Hive was built?' asked Moss.

'As far as I could tell, most of our kind fled. Many were sad, but a few were ready for a new adventure. A few tried to hang on for as long as they could – in parks, for example, or the bigger gardens, but all over the Hive the last really special places were being left without Hidden Folk to look after them, so I decided to do what I could.

'I found an ancient, wizened thorn tree, the last remnant of what had once been a shady, winding lane looked after by one of our kind, called Blewit, who had decided to leave the Hive. What had been a faint deer track through the undergrowth, then a path trodden by Mortals, became a lane when they began to travel on horses, and it stayed that way for eight hundred cuckoo summers. Three lovely young hawthorn trees grew by the wayside, and May blossom and cow parsley made it beautiful in spring.

'This lane once led to a village, but eventually the village grew, so instead of running between hedges, the lane ran between houses, first of timber and later of brick. At last the Mortals' Hive, which had been in the distance, spread so close it gobbled the village up, and then the lane became a cobbled street with hundreds of other streets just like it all around.

'And then one day a Mortal decided to build a grand iron gateway for her house, and the funny little thorn tree was in the way. So down it came one autumn morning, with just a few blows of an axe – as though it didn't matter, as though in winter hungry thrushes didn't need its bright red berries, and in spring no bees relied on the nectar in its creamy blossoms for food.'

Cumulus's voice had become broken and halting. 'I'd scurried behind a heap of horse-dung while I tried to think what to do. When the Mortal raised his axe, I – I ran out to try and stop him. Pan knows, it all happened so fast. It was such a foolish, useless thing to do.'

They all sat quietly for a moment.

'Is that when you lost your eye?' Sorrel asked, in a gentle voice.

'Yes, though I was lucky: if the axe had touched me I'd have died, iron being fatal to Hidden Folk. When the Mortal began to drag away the tree that lay on top of me, I scrambled up and ran. I didn't even realize that I'd been hit by the falling branches – I suppose because I was so frightened, and my heart was banging so fast.'

'Cumulus, can I ask you something?' said Sorrel, hesitantly.

'Of course – anything you like.'

'You're the oldest of us, and you seem to know a lot about most things. I just wondered: have you ever seen Pan?'

'Oh, no – I don't think many wild creatures have – certainly not for hundreds and hundreds of cuckoo summers, anyway. But we see Pan in the skies in autumn, don't we? The three stars of the belt, and then the pipe that hangs from it; two upstretched hands, like ours, and two strong hooves. Those stars are a reminder that we're protected through the cold months, and they watch over us during our winter sleep.'

'Yes, but . . . how do you know Pan's *real*? I mean, we say "Pan alive" and "Pan's teeth" and things like that all the time, but perhaps Pan is a – a story we've been telling ourselves – a good one, a useful one, because whether they're true or not, stories teach us things, but—'

'Nobody can ever be completely sure, I suppose,' interrupted Burnet, a little irritably. 'Pan just *feels* real to me – and anyway, I don't like this kind of talk.'

'Why not?' said Sorrel.

'Because . . . because I just don't. If Pan wasn't real, it would mean that we're alone in the Wild World, with nobody looking after us, and I – I don't like that feeling at all!'

Sorrel reached out and squeezed Burnet's hand. 'I know what you mean, Burnet. But the things that give us uncomfy feelings are exactly the kind of things we *should* be talking about.'

'That's all right for you to say, Sorrel, you're not the one disappearing,' replied Burnet, whose voice was a little unsteady. 'I'm scared, so I don't want to feel doubt or worry about things at the moment. I just want everything to be simple, and clear, and – and ordinary.'

Cumulus spoke kindly: 'Things aren't simple or clear at the moment, Burnet. I'm disappearing too, and I don't mind admitting that I'm frightened. None of us knows what's wrong, and none of us can be sure what'll happen next – any more than we can be sure Pan is real and watches over us. But lots of things in life aren't certain, and there's no point pretending otherwise.'

Burnet sniffled a little. 'I didn't know you were frightened, Cumulus. I thought it was just me.'

'Oh, dear, I did wonder if I should have mentioned it. I thought it was best if I put a brave face on how I felt, being the oldest – even though I didn't want to. I kept wanting a hug, you know, but I made myself push the feeling down so I could look brave. I'm really sorry if you thought you were the only one who was worried. That must have been ever so lonely for you.'

Burnet shuffled over a bit in the magpie's nest and the two friends gave each other a long hug. It was one of those hugs that has so many warm feelings in it that it actually heals both the huggers a little bit. Both of them were smiling, and had their eyes closed. Watching them, Moss's heart felt full; what a fine thing it was to have friends who were so kind and honest, and to know that it was all right to have wobbly feelings now and then.

'Anyway. After that I didn't want to be in the Mortals' Hive any more,' said Cumulus once the hug was over and they had all found a comfortable sitting position again. 'I joined the wandering bands of Hidden Folk who trudged through the Wild World, looking for a home. And after a while I got used to only seeing out of one eye – though, as you know, I still can't judge distance very well. And eventually I met you two, stirring a walnut-shell of hot sloe jam by a row of young ash trees in a hedgerow' – here Cumulus smiled at Moss and Burnet – 'and you kindly took me in.'

'Gosh,' said Moss. 'And to think we never realized what you had gone through – or that you'd been to the Mortals' Hive. Is it very different nowadays? I suppose it must be.'

'Well, it's packed with death-chariots now, of course,' Cumulus replied. 'That's a big change. Beyond that, I don't know yet.'

Sorrel spoke up, a little haltingly. 'I was just wondering . . . I mean, it's probably nothing. But if there are any Hidden Folk still living in the Hive, wouldn't the pigeons know of it? There are lots of them here, and they can fly and everything, but I'm pretty sure we came as a total surprise to them.'

'I was thinking that as well,' replied Moss, and Burnet nodded too.

'Well, hopefully we'll find out more tomorrow,' said Cumulus. 'Speaking of which, we should really get some shut-eye, or we'll be of no use to bird nor beast.'

So the four Hidden Folk unpacked their spider-silk sleeping bags and laid them out close to one another in the old magpie's nest. Then they got in, curled up all warm and cosy, closed their eyes and waited for sleep.

Not far away roosted the four trusty pigeons, and above them hung the black velvet of the night sky; down below lay the vast and wakeful city, teeming with wild creatures and twinkling with lights.

17

The takeaway

*The four make a new
friend ... and lose one
of their number.*

The four Hidden Folk were woken just before
sunrise by the sound of city birdsong, as robins,
blackbirds, wrens and great tits belted out their
different tunes. All four had slept extremely well in
the twiggy magpie's nest, despite the unfamiliar
sound of traffic; in fact, the constant rumbling
seemed to have helped them drift off.

'Morning, everyone!' said Moss, sitting up and
stretching in the dimness. The sky beyond the plane
tree's sheltering leaves was still velvety blue, but in
the east, where the sun rose, it was flushing salmon
pink. 'D'you know, I didn't think there'd be a dawn
chorus in the Mortals' Hive. It feels like a lovely
start to our visit, don't you think?'

'It does, doesn't it.' said Burnet. 'I can't hear as
many different birds as there were by the Folly, but

on the other hand it almost sounds as though they're singing more loudly here.'

'Perhaps they are,' replied Moss. 'You know – to make sure they can be heard properly over all the other noise.'

'So strange to think that by the time it's summer the dawn chorus will be over for another year,' said Sorrel. 'Do you know, as long as I've lived, I've never really got used to that.'

'I wonder where we'll be when autumn comes,' mused Moss. 'Still in the Mortals' Hive, or back at the Folly with Sorrel? Or somewhere else entirely?'

'Cumulus, are you awake?' said Burnet. 'Where do *you* think we'll be come autumn time?'

'I'm awake,' came a voice from deep inside one of the sleeping bags. 'I haven't come out, because – well, I might as well tell you all. It's hard to be sure, but I think most of me's disappeared.'

Moss gasped, and reached for Burnet's hand.

'It's all right,' continued Cumulus, in a slightly shaky voice. 'It doesn't hurt, and I'm still here, just about. It's just that – well, I think I might look a bit peculiar, and I thought you should be prepared.'

'Come out, dear friend,' said Sorrel, whose voice also shook a little. 'It'll be all right, I promise.'

'Are you ready?'

Moss nodded, despite feeling really frightened.

'We're ready,' said Burnet.

Emerging from the sleeping bag came a wisp of long white hair so faint as to look like a trick of the light. After it came Cumulus's long, green robe; no hands protruded from the sleeves, of course; and it was long enough to cover Cumulus's invisible feet.

Moss blinked very hard and squeezed Burnet's hand. Immediately they realized how beloved Cumulus's face was to them, and how much they missed it already. Would they ever see it again? Was the same thing going to happen to all of them – and who would be next?

'Could we – could we hug you?' asked Moss.

The arms of the robe reached out wide. 'Oh, of course! I'd love that,' Cumulus cried.

All three felt better once they had hugged Cumulus and felt that their friend was still there. They held hands and laughed, and Burnet, who was extra frightened, cried a bit and then kicked Cumulus's invisible legs with an invisible foot, and Cumulus shouted 'Ow!' and poked Burnet in the belly with an invisible finger, and things didn't seem quite so bad after that.

'Just make sure you keep looking at me, as far as is possible. I'm still here, all right?' said Cumulus.

The others promised that they always, *always* would.

The pigeons were still sleeping, four fat balls of feathers silhouetted among the branches. Given how far they had flown the previous day, everyone agreed that they could probably do with a rest. But just as the Hidden Folk were finishing their breakfast, Roger opened his golden eye and shook out his dark feathers, and Rani woke up too and stretched out her barred wings.

'Only three of you?' asked Rani. 'Where's the wrinkly one gone?' Beside her, the other two urban pigeons were instantly awake.

'I'm here,' said Cumulus, waving an invisible arm in its green sleeve. 'Sorry about this. I can't help it.'

'Ooh, you didn't half give us a fright,' said Ron. 'I thought you'd fallen out of the tree! As long as you're still all right, your appearance is your own affair. We've seen more surprising things than an empty robe in the Hive – isn't that right, Reni?'

'I take it you didn't save any breakfast for your feathered friends?' said Roger, seeing that the Hidden Folk had finished eating. 'Typical!'

'Let's go and find something – I'm starving,' said Rani.

'Can we come?' asked Sorrel.

174

'Best not, or you'll be seen by a Mortal – well, not Cumulus, but the other three of you might,' replied Roger. 'There's an old lady who feeds us seeds every morning in a little park not far away. Back soon!' And with that, all four launched themselves from their branch and were gone.

'Did you hear that?' asked Burnet, turning to the others. 'That's the second time someone's mentioned that Mortals actually feed birds, on purpose. They never did that in our old garden, did they, Moss?'

'No, but I think the Mortal girl next door might have.' Moss often thought about Ro, and wondered what she was up to and whether she spoke the Wild Argot to any of the birds and animals in her garden. 'She seemed to really like wild creatures – do you remember?'

'At one time, lots of Mortals kept birds in cages, and they must have fed those ones,' Cumulus mused. 'Mostly, though, I remember them chasing birds away from their farms and fields, trapping them, stealing their eggs and shooting them dead with firesticks. If some of them have started feeding them now, that sounds like a very good thing!'

The four Hidden Folk sat with their legs dangling over the edge of the magpie's nest as the sky got light and around them the busy city began a new day. Their plane tree grew on a pavement next to a road along which buses, cars, taxis, scooters and cyclists soon began to stream. There was a pedestrian crossing, which made a beeping noise to tell people when it was safe to cross, and the top halves of the buildings had people living in them, while at ground level were shops and businesses: there were newsagents and off-licenses, mobile-phone repair shops and grocers with piles of brightly coloured exotic fruit, a small supermarket, a shop selling discount handbags, which still had its shutters down, a Polish bakery, a greasy-spoon café, a locksmith and a boarded-up pub. The pavement directly under them was dotted with blackened chewing-gum, and a little further away there was a kiosk where it was sold, along with newspapers, magazines and brightly wrapped snacks.

It felt so strange to Moss to be sitting up there while Mortals passed so close below. Some pushed buggies or held the hands of Mortal children in school uniform; many of them held little black slabs which lit up when they touched them, and which they stared at a lot. Quite a few had dogs, and not all of them were on leads, which wasn't good.

'This is a bit scary, isn't it?' said Moss after a while.

'What if one of them were to look up and see us?'

'Oh, don't y'all worry about *that*,' came a voice from the branches below. 'They're hardly dangerous at all, these Hive-dwellers! Most of the time I just do *'zactly* – as – I – please.'

With those words, a squirrel's beady, inquisitive face popped up, right between Burnet's bare, dangling legs.

'Aieeeee!' screamed Burnet, shooting backwards into the nest with fright.

'And *that* is why you won't ever catch me wearing a kilt,' laughed Sorrel.

'Hey, fairies!' said the squirrel, hauling himself into the nest and grinning at them all. 'I'm Chip. Pleased to make your acquaintance.'

'Excuse me, but we are *not* fairies!' said Burnet, who had just about recovered, but was still a bit flustered. '*Everyone* knows that fairies turned into songbirds long, long ago.'

'Oh, I do beg your joint and collective pardons,' said Chip, absentmindedly grooming his magnificent fluffy tail. 'I assumed you were, what with you being tiny, and the fact that you must've flown up into this here tree. But if you're not fairies, what in the Wild World *are* you – particularly the one of you that ain't all there?'

Burnet spoke up. 'We're Hidden Folk, and we didn't fly here. As you'd see if you looked, we're completely wingless. We got a lift from some very kind pigeons.'

'Oh, *pigeons*!' said Chip. 'I can't abide 'em, the greedy so-and-sos. Always eating all the rations the Mortals kindly put out for me.'

Burnet was about to say something to that, but Moss's elbow shot out in a hard nudge.

'So I take it you haven't seen any more of our people living here in the Hive?' asked Cumulus.

'Not in all my born days, good golly, no. Mind you, my kind ain't been here long compared to our little ginger cousins – not that we see much of them any more, for which I am heartily sorry, I'm sure I am. No, you're a new one on me, and that's a fact. Why, are y'all looking for someone?'

So Cumulus told Chip the story of their quest, and how they feared that the rest of their kind might have disappeared, and how they had heard tell of more Hidden Folk in the Mortals' Hive, as unlikely as that might sound. When the story was over, Chip didn't look quite so chipper any more.

'Want me to ask around? Me and my partner Bud, we know everyone in this street. We know all the other squirrels, of course – and there sure are a *lot* of us! – the parakeets, a fair few ladybirds, a couple of bats – you know, the little squeaky ones – Terry the turtle, who a Mortal put in the big pond a few streets over, a coupla crows, a few hice mice – sorry, house mouses – all the sparrows . . . Bud swears he used to know an actual hedgehog once, but he's – well. Between you, me and the fencepost, he got squished.'

Everyone's faces took on a solemn expression for a moment. Once upon a time they had all had hedgehog friends, but it was a bit like red squirrels: hardly anyone saw them any more.

'Being squished is the biggest danger here,' continued Chip. 'But stay out of buildings and off the roads and the full-grown Mortals'll barely see you; they're all too busy to notice us much, and that's a fact. As for the little ones, I find some of 'em see me, some just . . . don't. Me 'n' Bud once built a drey in a poplar tree next to an apartment block and a little boy used to watch us all the time through one of the windows. We used to chase each other around the trunk just to make him laugh. It sure was fun!'

'Thank you, that's reassuring. And we'll definitely be careful of the death-chariots,' Cumulus said.

'Anyway, want me to ask around? If there really are any of your lot living in the Hive, someone'll know about it, for sure. Where can I find you all? Are you planning to set up home in this here tree?'

'Well, that's still a bit . . . up in the air at the moment, if you'll pardon the pun,' said Moss. 'When the pigeons get back, we're going to ask them for a lift down, and then we're hoping to find somewhere safe and quiet to stay.'

'Safe and quiet? *Safe - and - quiet?*' said Chip, breaking into a strange laugh that sounded a bit like a sneezing duck. 'Hooey, no – here in the Hive those two ain't the same thing at all. If you want safe, you don't want quiet. Pick somewhere busy and well-lit, that's my advice. And with good scavenging potential, too.'

'Scavenging for what?' asked Moss, who was still hungry.

'Mortal food!' said Chip. 'Don't go telling me you haven't ever tried it?'

'I tasted some of their gruel once,' said Sorrel. 'It must have been . . . ooh, hundreds of cuckoo summers ago. Horrible, it was. Give me a nice bowl of snail porridge any day.'

'Oh, they've got a lot better at cooking since the olden days of yore,' said Chip. '*Gee whizz!* You wouldn't believe how sweet and salty their food is these days. I mean, no creature with half a brain would want to actually *live* on it, but if you just have some now and again, it can't be beat.'

Moss eyed the squirrel's white-furred belly. It looked a lot like he ate Mortal food every day.

'So where can we find it, Chip?'

'Oh, that's easy – they waste such a lot, these Hive-dwellers. And I think I know just the place.'

At lunchtime the four friends were cautiously exploring a little park next to a bus stop that was bustling with wild creatures of all kinds. Dandelions had been allowed to grow around the edges and were being visited by bees, as was the white dead-nettle, which looks like a stinging nettle but doesn't sting, and buddleia, a shrub with long purple flower spikes that had arrived here from China with the help of Mortals and was a favourite with butterflies. There was a tangly, unmown part which was full of grasshoppers and shield bugs, there were benches for Mortals to sit on near a play area, some bins and – as a couple of the local children knew very well – an excellent climbing tree with low branches to haul yourself on to and a good sitting spot further up. From the bushes came the wheezy, insistent sound of newly fledged birds still demanding to be fed, while high above the Hive swifts let out their summer-sounding screams.

Under one of the benches, Moss and Sorrel had crept right inside a cardboard takeaway box and were blissfully tucking into some jerk chicken. The intense, spicy taste was completely unfamiliar, and they both absolutely loved it. Meanwhile, Burnet and Cumulus had also discovered something new.

'Is this food?' asked Burnet, poking a French fry, cautiously. 'It doesn't look like food.'

'Smells like it, though,' said Cumulus, invisibly breaking off the brownest and crispiest end, which glittered with salt. 'Let's try a bit. Oh, my goodness. *Oh, dear Pan.* Burnet, you need to try this. I think it's potato, but . . .'

'Potato? Sounds boring.'

'Honestly, try it. It's like a potato that someone's done magic on!'

As the two of them began to nibble the French fry, one at each end, the four pigeons fluttered down.

'We're off now. We know where you'll be, so if we hear anything about your kind, we'll come and find you,' promised Roger.

'And even if not, I'll nip back now and again,' said Rani kindly. 'Just in case you decide you're ready to be airlifted out.'

And then they were away, spiralling up into the blue city skies, dipping once for a synchronized loop-the-loop and then disappearing from sight. Just for a moment, Moss's heart soared with them, remembering the wonderful freedom of flight.

Once they had all finished eating, they crawled into their tents, well camouflaged under the rhododendron, for a nap. Their first real taste of human food had proved overwhelming, and they all needed to sleep it off. Some burps and other impolite digestive sounds could be heard issuing from some of the tiny tents, and at least one of the Hidden Folk, stuffed full of jerk chicken, had rather a bad case of the meat sweats.

When Moss woke up, it was early evening, which in summer is the warmest time of day in most Hives: the sunshine gets trapped by all the buildings and tarmac and builds up as the day goes on. The other Hidden Folk were still asleep and snoring, and Moss, whose tummy was rumbling, decided it would be unkind to wake them. How dangerous could it really be to go for a little mosey about and see if there might be more of that delicious Mortal food anywhere?

'I've learnt a lot on our journey,' thought Moss. 'I think I'm ready to go on a tiny solo recce now.'

In one direction lay a flower bed planted with bright flowers, then the bus stop and the busy road – and Moss hadn't forgotten Chip's warning about its dangers. But if you went the other way, there was grass starred with dandelions and daisies, and beyond that the playground and the benches, which was where the bins were. Moss strolled that way, keeping under cover and listening to the thin, silvery evening song of a robin perched in a tree somewhere nearby.

It seemed so silly now, how terrified they'd all been of the Mortals' Hive. How dangerous they had imagined it was, and how bleak and dirty, with no birdsong or flowers – but how wrong they'd been! Even Mortals weren't as frightening as all that, really – not when you got used to them being absolutely everywhere, and you realized how little notice they took of things. It was extraordinary, really, Moss thought, the way Mortals went unheedingly about their business, as though all the fascinating, intricate and ongoing dramas of the creaturely world didn't exist – as though all the friendships and battles, the gluttonous feasts and tragic deaths of the animals and birds, the creepy-crawlies and Hidden Folk around them were utterly invisible. Honestly, one might as well just strut around in the open for all the—

When the cat pounced it was utterly instantaneous, and made Moss's world wink out like a light. Gripped between sharp white teeth, the limp little body was taken, in just a few bounds, out of the park and away.

18

Determination

Spangle has a plan.

The world doesn't stop when something terrible happens. One of the most awful things about tragedy is the way everything just . . . carries on. Mortals, young and old, continued to walk through the little park, their feet passing only a couple of metres from the four tiny tents camouflaged among the dead leaves under a rhododendron bush. On the busy road the buses and taxis kept on driving by, and darkness continued to fall.

If only this chapter could begin by describing how Moss was quickly dropped by the cat, or managed to struggle and yell and somehow get away. If only this story could be about the others waking up and wondering where on earth their dear friend was, and feeling increasingly worried; and then, at last, Moss could appear at the campsite, perhaps missing that silly acorn-cup hat, a little shaken, but unhurt.

But sadly, that isn't what happened. That isn't what happened at all.

It was Sorrel who woke up first, and then Burnet. They sat and talked in quiet voices, sitting on two plastic bottle caps and a cork, which Sorrel had cut in half so that the four of them each had a small, round stool. Eventually Cumulus joined them, yawning audibly.

'Moss not up yet? That's unusual.'

'Must be having a lie-in,' said Burnet.

'It'll be all that spicy chicken!' laughed Sorrel. 'I've never seen anyone eat so much.'

And so they sat and chatted about this and that, all the while getting accustomed to the life of the little park going on all around them, so different from life on the banks of the Folly, or in an ordinary garden: Mortals walking by singly and in groups, some laughing, some making the sound that among their kind passed for singing; the smells of all sorts of delicious food, sirens wailing over the traffic, headlights sweeping past, a dog barking, the *beep-beep-beep* of the pedestrian crossing, the last joyful screams of swifts fading away in the darkening sky overhead. Somewhere in the little park the robin was still giving his evening recital, but eventually he fell silent, having found somewhere safe to roost for the night.

'I'm going to wake Moss up,' said Cumulus at last, getting up. 'It's possible to sleep *too much*, you know.'

There was a pause. Then, a moment later:

'Burnet! Sorrel! Oh, come quickly – look, the tent is empty! Moss is *gone!*'

Burnet realized straight away that whatever had happened to Moss could happen to the rest of them, and that they were all in danger of getting lost by rushing out to search in the dark. On expeditions, it's panic that poses the greatest danger, because common sense goes out of the window and people act in ways they wouldn't otherwise. So, despite their terrible worry, the three remaining Hidden Folk stayed in Moss's tent until morning, hugging one another and crying.

'Moss has probably just gone for a walk, and made a new friend,' Sorrel offered at one point. 'You know what it's like: you get talking, you don't notice the time passing . . . like when you first met Eddy the otter, you know?'

But the other two knew that Moss would never in a million years have made them worry like this; not unless something awful had occurred.

'Chip'll be here in the morning,' Burnet said, not for the first time. 'He'll have a plan for how to find Moss, I'm sure of it. Chip'll know what to do.'

But it wasn't the squirrel who came to the four little tents at first light. Just as the sky began to grow pale and the first bird tried a tentative note, there was a fast clicking sound, a lot like someone tapping very quickly on wood, and then a 'BING-BONG!' exactly like a doorbell.

'All right, Bosses, where you at?' came Spangle the starling's unmistakeable voice.

The trio tumbled out of Moss's tent, falling over one another in their haste to tell the startled bird the news.

'And we didn't dare go looking in the dark, but, honestly, we're beside ourselves – just tell us, Spangle, what should we do?' concluded Burnet.

Spangle looked grave. 'This is a bad business. A very bad business,' he said, shaking his head. 'I hope Moss ain't got murked.'

'Does that mean . . . do you think . . . ?' said Cumulus, and then stopped, not quite able to say the words out loud.

'No point thinking like that,' said the bird. 'What we gotta do is look. Moss could be lying hurt somewhere. I'll round up my crew; Cumulus: you stay here and wait for this squirrel of yours. Burnet and Sorrel, go and search on foot – but stay in the park and stick together, you get me?'

So that is what they did. Spangle quickly returned with seven other starlings, who wheeled in a flock around the park and the pavements, their beady black eyes alert for anything amiss. Burnet and Sorrel began to search at ground level, looking under dead leaves and crisp packets and calling out, 'Moss! Moss?' as they went. Chip, when he appeared, fetched Bud, and the two of them scoured everything that was climbable, turning birds rudely out of their nests to check for injured Hidden Folk, diving into smelly litter bins and even scaling nearby buildings to look in the gutters and on the roofs.

At first Cumulus hated having to stay by the tents, but as more and more of the park's inhabitants heard the commotion, they arrived there asking how they could help – keen too, no doubt, to get a look at a real live member of the Hidden Folk, because word had travelled and none of them had ever seen one before. That day sparked a mistaken belief, still widespread among some city-dwelling creatures, that all Hidden Folk are more or less invisible. For quite a few of the park's inhabitants, Cumulus was the first and only example they would ever come across.

Cumulus coordinated the entire search operation, and turned out to be very good at it indeed. By the afternoon the entire park was in uproar, though to an unobservant child walking home from school, it might not have looked much different from usual, with birds flying from branch to branch and squirrels running across the grass. A noticing child, of course, would have spotted that the movements of the birds and animals weren't random, but had purpose and meaning. And, who knows, had they sat quietly for a while and watched, they might even have seen one of the Hidden Folk.

By early evening they had searched the entire park as well as the surrounding pavements and buildings, and there was still no sign of Moss. They met up under the rhododendron bushes to discuss what to do.

Cumulus, Burnet and Sorrel were exhausted, not to mention very worried and very sad. Nobody wanted to stop searching, but at some point they all knew they would need to rest. They weren't allowing themselves to think beyond the next few hours. The prospect of a future without their friend was too much to bear.

'We're not done yet,' said Spangle. 'We ain't asked the foxes. They'll be up and around soon as darkness comes. It was dark when Moss disappeared, right?

Stands to reason one of the night crew might know something.'

'But foxes are evil!' objected Bud.

'Oh my days. Evil? Who's been telling you that?'

'All right, all right – not *evil*. But they're predators!'

'True say, but that don't make 'em evil. There's no goodies and baddies in the Wild World – you know that, or you should do anyway. Everything's got to get by somehow – you lot, us birds, foxes, too. The Hidden Folk eat fishes and grasshoppers and whatnot, don't you? And I'm all about the bugs and worms, what would otherwise stay alive. You squirrels love an egg, or so I've heard; and even if you just stuck to acorns, you're stopping those acorns from growing up into a tree. It's not so simple, see?'

'Sure, but . . . a fox might eat us – or you!'

'Well, yeah, that's true, and I ain't saying I'd like it. Don't get me wrong: it's our job not to be eaten, just like it's their job to eat enough to stay alive. But that don't make 'em evil. Anyway, what choice do we have? We need help if we want to find out what's happened to Moss.'

'I say we trust them,' said Cumulus slowly. 'Spangle's right. We've got no choice.'

19

Moss

*In the darkest hour, there
is still laughter – and hope.*

The two squirrels sat with Spangle on a low
branch to wait for night to fall. It was particularly hard for the starling to stay awake; he kept
wanting to tuck his head under his wing. The
squirrels, too, looked drowsy; they weren't used to
staying up quite so late.

It grew dark, but there were still lots of Mortals
around; it wasn't like the countryside, where, apart
from a few silent hunters, the world became quiet
and still at night.

At last the moon rose high, the traffic slowed,
and the park emptied out. On the ground below,
Cumulus, Burnet and Sorrel tried not to think
about their friend who was, at best, lying injured
somewhere, enduring a second scary night alone in
the dark.

'Look!' whispered Burnet, whose eyes were a little sharper than the others'. Overhead, Chip squeezed Bud's paw, who stifled a squeak.

There at the edge of the park a sleek shape had appeared. Silent-footed and dim in the streetlight, bushy tail held out behind, it trotted past the children's play area, paused for a moment to sniff at a discarded chicken bone and crunched it up, showing strong white teeth. Then it raised its neat muzzle to show the white fur of its chin, and sniffed the air.

'I don't like this . . .' whispered Sorrel. In the countryside foxes are rarely seen, and are much less bold; being this close to one felt very alarming.

'*Zip it*,' said Spangle, quite loudly. Then: 'Here goes,' he muttered, and fluttered over to where the fox was.

Everyone's hearts thumped, and Chip buried his face in his paws, saying, 'I can't look!'

Spangle landed on the tarmac path in front of the fox, which lowered its head and brush and pointed its triangular ears forward. They appeared to be communicating, though no sound could be heard.

'When it comes to foxes, the Wild Argot becomes very mysterious,' Cumulus whispered. 'A lot of it is done through body language – particularly the ears and tail, and that intense gaze they have.'

After a few moments Spangle flew back to the others. He seemed elated by the risk he had taken.

'She says to come over – we can trust her,' he said, a little breathlessly; instead of frightened, he looked more than a little starry-eyed. 'Her name's Vesper, and she's curious to meet you. Don't worry, I've warned her about your, erm . . . y'know. The invisible thing. Everyone just – *be polite.*'

The moment they were looking up at the vixen's beautiful golden eyes, they all found that they could communicate quite easily – just as they had with Fleet, Sven, Eddy and all the other wild creatures they'd met.

Spangle had explained the situation already. Now, pointing her ears forward and tipping her head to one side, Vesper asked the three friends to tell her everything they could about Moss, from appearance (here they mentioned the acorn-cup hat) to character ('More of an indoor person,' said Cumulus; 'Quite greedy,' said Burnet, which Sorrel corrected to, 'Appreciates fine cuisine'). Then she bent her head and asked if she might sniff them, so as to understand and remember the particular smell of their kind. Chip and Bud, who had kept several paces back, squeaked and huddled together, trembling, as the trio closed their eyes in the darkness and allowed the fox's nose to pass carefully around them, inhaling their smell.

It was done. Vesper promised them that after she had hunted she would spend the rest of the night looking for Moss – and that she would also ask her kind if any of them had caught anything unusual recently. Although it was a horrible thought, it would, Cumulus agreed, be better to know.

The squirrels left for their drey, and Spangle roosted deep in the rhododendron bush above the encampment, promising not to do any droppings in his sleep. But, despite being exhausted, Cumulus, Burnet and Sorrel couldn't seem to drop off.

It was Sorrel who eventually found the courage to begin the conversation that, at some point, they needed to have. Perhaps it was a bit easier for a newcomer to the group than for the other two, who had been friends with Moss for so many hundreds of years.

'What if – what if we never find Moss?' Sorrel

whispered at last. 'What will we do then – will we leave the Hive?'

There was a long silence. Sorrel knew that Cumulus and Burnet were still awake in their tents because their breathing hadn't yet slowed, or turned into snores.

'I – I don't know,' said Cumulus at last. 'The thought of carrying on without our dear, dear friend is unbearable . . . but I don't know if I could bear to stay here, in the Hive. We came to look for answers, and hopefully find more of our kind – not lose them.'

'Well, if you wanted to live with me beside the Folly, Hetty and I would love to have you,' said Sorrel. 'Even if you both vanish completely, you'll always be welcome. I hope you don't mind me saying that. I just wanted to make sure you knew.'

'That's so kind of you, Sorrel,' said Burnet. 'You are a good friend, and we must always stick together now – whatever happens next, and wherever we go.'

All was quiet for a while. The lights of a plane making its final descent to the airport appeared in the sky and gradually passed overhead with a faint roar, while hundreds of kilometres above the teeming city the International Space Station travelled on its stately circuit around planet Earth, a bright white pinprick moving eastwards against the starry backdrop of the night.

'Hey, do you remember the thing with the toad spawn?' came Burnet's voice, after a while.

There was a snort of laughter from somewhere deep in Cumulus's tent.

'What toad spawn?' asked Sorrel.

'Oh, Sorrel, it was *so* silly,' said Burnet.

'And so like Moss!' added Cumulus.

'Tell me, one of you!'

'Well,' said Burnet, 'it was like this. Cumulus had just arrived at the ash tree – this was back when it was one of a row of ash trees in a hedge, not part of a garden, of course. How long had you been with us, Cumulus?'

'Oh, a day or so, two days – no more than that.'

'So we hadn't yet really got to know one another, and we were still all being terribly polite – you know how it is when you're trying to make friends. Anyway, we'd both seen how tired and sad Cumulus was (and, of course, now we understand why). So Moss had the idea of preparing a big feast and inviting lots of the Hedge People, to cheer Cumulus up. You know what Moss was like about food.'

'*Is* like,' said Cumulus gently.

'*Is* like. Yes – of course. Well, anyway' – voice

cracking a little, Burnet hurried on with the tale –
'the evening of the feast came, and all our neighbours arrived: a pair of hedgehogs, three hazel
dormice, five yellowhammers, some stag beetles,
Jenny Wren, Toady and Toadina McToadface, an
entire gang of wood mice—'

'*Very* greedy,' interjected Cumulus.

'Yes, they were, weren't they?' agreed Burnet.
'Anyway. There we all were, gathered at the base of
our hollow ash tree for our feast, with two dozen
specially invited glow-worms for light. Oh, yes, it
was *very* fancy. We were nibbling on watermint to
clear our palates between courses when in came
Moss, looking triumphant, carrying an absolutely
massive cauldron of – of—' And here Burnet dissolved
into helpless giggles, and couldn't talk any more.

'What?' cried Sorrel. 'What was it?!'

'Well,' said Cumulus, picking up the story. 'Moss
said it was poppy-seed jelly – a rare delicacy, apparently, and *extremely* difficult to make. And someone
asked for the recipe – was it Jenny Wren, Burnet?'

'Oh, yes, I think it was her,' replied Burnet.

'Anyway, Moss – who had gone as red as a lobster
– began to explain how it was made, but it was so
complicated that nobody could follow it, and it went
on for ages and I remember thinking – even though

I'd only known both of you for a couple of days – I remember thinking, "That somehow doesn't sound like a real recipe – it sounds a bit made up!" And then – and then—'

'And then Toady tried some, and it was all – all *stringy* – and the look on his face!'

'And then he nudged Toadina, didn't he? And she stared at the jelly and went a bit cross-eyed, because—'

'Oh, no. *Oh, no* – it wasn't, was it?' asked Sorrel. 'Surely it wasn't. Tell me it wasn't!'

But all Cumulus and Burnet could do was laugh helplessly, tears streaming from their eyes, and splutter, 'It was!' 'It was!'

It took a long time for the three of them to stop laughing. Every time it subsided, one of them would say 'toad spawn!' and set the others off again, or there would come a distant snort of laughter from one of the tents and they would all become mildly hysterical again. Sorrel kept begging them to stop, saying, 'Oh, oh, oh, it's making my tummy hurt!' – but somehow that was funny too, and just kept the joke going.

'Oh, Pan, *please*,' said Burnet in the end. 'I can't laugh any more, I'll *die*.'

'No more laughing, absolutely,' said Cumulus. 'Not a single snort. Agreed.'

'I just . . . I don't understand,' said Sorrel. 'Where on earth did Moss get it from?'

'Oh, well it turns out an unscrupulous badger brought news of it, in exchange for a big pile of hazelnuts from our stores. You know how much badgers like nuts of any kind.'

'And so . . . did Moss know that it was toad spawn?'

'Oh, no – the badger had said he knew of some rare, valuable poppy-seed jelly, and explained that it was in a nearby pond. Pan only knows why Moss believed him; it was a ridiculous story, really.'

'Perhaps it was just a case of getting caught up in preparing for the feast, and wanting it all to be perfect,' said Sorrel.

'Yes, that sounds like Moss,' said Cumulus. 'And it was a lovely party, apart from the slight awkwardness about dessert. I felt very welcome indeed.'

'And do you remember the ballad?'

'After dinner? Of course. Oh, it was wonderful, Sorrel – those ballads always were, though I wish now I'd told Moss that more often. But this one had been adapted at the last minute to include the news of my arrival.'

'Oh, how kind and thoughtful!' exclaimed Sorrel. 'Do you know, I haven't heard a proper ballad in a hundred cuckoo summers. I remember a few of the old ones; I didn't know any of our kind still made them, until I met Moss. Now I wish I'd asked to hear one.'

'I don't think this year's ballad is ready yet,' said Cumulus. 'But one day, when we're reunited with Moss – Pan willing – we'll all sit down together and hear the story of our adventures told properly, and it will be every bit as good as the famous ones. Because I'll tell you something: there's far more talent under that little wooden cap than our friend knows.'

20

Friend or foe?

*Help can sometimes come from
the most unexpected direction.*

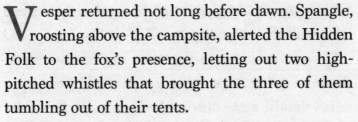

Vesper returned not long before dawn. Spangle, roosting above the campsite, alerted the Hidden Folk to the fox's presence, letting out two high-pitched whistles that brought the three of them tumbling out of their tents.

The vixen looked grave. She hadn't found Moss, she told them straight away, but she did have news – and it wasn't good. One of her brothers had come across something unusual early the previous morning. He'd led her to a spot just a few streets away, and there, lying on a pavement – unremarkable to anyone without a wild creature's sense of smell – was Moss's acorn-cup hat. It was cracked, and missing its jaunty stem.

'And – you're sure?' asked Burnet, whose voice was trembling. 'I mean, there must be acorn cups and oak galls and twigs and dead leaves and all kinds of tree frass all over the Mortals' Hive. Who's to say this one particular acorn cup was Moss's?'

Vesper lowered her eyes.

'The smell,' said Burnet, haltingly. 'Yes, of course. It smelt to you – of *us*.'

That wasn't all it smelt of, though, she told them; and that was the worst part of the story. The wooden cap also smelt of cat.

'Will you take us to where you found it, please?' asked Burnet urgently. 'Now – straight away? Before all the Mortals get up?'

Vesper lay down on the grass so that they could climb on to her back, and then carefully stood up.

It was still quite dim in the little park. From the trees and bushes, the birds were singing the dawn chorus, but the sun hadn't yet risen high enough above the city's buildings to give much light. They all knew that they didn't have long – and none of them wanted to be out on the busy streets for long after daybreak.

In the bush above them, Spangle puffed out his feathers and gave them a good shake. 'Oh my days,' he said. 'Well, if we're *really* doing this, I might as well be lookout, so keep an ear out for my whistle. Vesper, lead the way!'

And so they stole through the waking city in the half-light, Vesper slipping sleek between parked cars, trotting along the alleyways between houses and sidling past tall wheelie bins on silent paws. On a dark street a tabby cat hissed at them, puffing out its fur and arching its back before slinking away to a waiting cat flap. The three Hidden Folk were terrified, but Vesper didn't pause. On they went, as all around them Mortals snored and slumbered in their warm beds, the time on their phones counting down to the moment when their alarms would go off.

When the fox stopped and let them climb down, they found themselves beside a tall, white block of flats that stood at one corner of a big crossroads. A strip of green grass ran around it, separated from the pavement by a square privet hedge. Spangle immediately alighted on top, his bright, beady eyes looking all around.

Delicately, Vesper lowered her muzzle and indicated an acorn cup that lay near the hedge. Burnet picked it up and looked inside. A tiny 'M' could just about be seen.

'I remember poor Moss scratching that with my knife,' whispered Burnet.

Just then, the door of the flats opened and a man

came out with a muscular dog on a lead. Spangle barely had time to let out a sharp whistle before the dog pulled the man through a gap in the privet and on to the pavement, sending the Hidden Folk scrambling for cover under the hedge. They crouched there together, trembling, as the dog sniffed eagerly in their direction, and Burnet tucked Moss's cap safely away.

'Don't worry – it can't reach us,' hissed Sorrel. 'The Mortal's holding on to it. I see dogs now and again at the Folly – they're usually all right, as long as they're not running free.'

Although they didn't know it, the dog, a Staffordshire bull terrier, was very friendly and loving – as that breed tends to be, unless badly treated. All the same, most birds and animals are easily startled by dogs, which is why it's kindest to keep them on the lead around wild creatures.

'I still don't like it,' muttered Burnet – and just then, the grinning dog cocked its leg, and did a wee. Fortunately, they all jumped back in time.

When the dog had gone, led away by its oblivious owner, Cumulus, Burnet and Sorrel tiptoed out from the other side of the hedge, away from the pavement and towards the flats.

'Where's Vesper?' asked Burnet – but, frightened

by the Staffie, the shy russet fox was nowhere to be seen.

'Oh no,' said Sorrel. 'Now we're stuck here! Quick, Burnet, let's you and I scout around for somewhere we can hide for a while – somewhere away from dogs.'

'And I'll have a fly about, see if I can see Vesper,' said Spangle. 'She won't have gone far, I don't reckon.'

So Cumulus was all alone when, some moments later, a high-pitched voice emanated from a dim grating at the bottom of the white building.

'Oi!' it said. 'Oi, you, Mister Invisible. Lost a mate, 'ave you?'

Centuries later, when recalling their adventures, Cumulus would describe hearing that whisper as a breath of chill, cold fear. Despite everything that was to happen from that moment onwards, hindsight never erased the memory, or stripped it of its terror. For there, emerging from the dark foundations of the building, were the sharp features of a rat.

'Come 'ere,' the black-eyed rodent whispered to Cumulus. '*Now.*'

Trembling a little, Cumulus did so. But just then, Burnet and Sorrel came back, arguing about whether a large, discarded crisp packet would make a good temporary hiding-place – and, quick as a flash, the rat's face disappeared.

'D-did you see that?' asked Cumulus.

'See what?' said Burnet.

'The rat – just now!'

'Rat? Where?' said Sorrel, looking around in all directions.

'In the grating. Just now.'

'No. Has it gone?' asked Burnet. 'Ugh, horrible things. I bet they're everywhere in these parts. What did it say to you? Did it want to catch you and bite you, do you think?'

'I – I don't know. I don't think so.'

'Oh, I wouldn't be surprised. They eat anything and everything, you know.'

'Well, at least you're all right,' said Sorrel, soothingly. 'Now, we've found some useful litter, well, *I* did really, and—'

'I think it knows something,' interrupted Cumulus. 'Something about Moss.'

'The rat, you mean?'

'Yes. It asked me if I had lost someone.'

Burnet shivered. 'That sounds creepy. I bet it was watching the three of us and saw me and Sorrel go off, and you left alone. Even more reason to find somewhere safe to wait for Vesper.'

'No – I don't think that was it. It wasn't laughing, or trying to sound scary. I really think it wanted to help.'

'Hmm, I doubt that very much, somehow,' said Burnet, who, despite never having met one, and not actually knowing the first thing about them, had very fixed ideas about rats.

Sorrel, though, was less easily influenced by what others said. Perhaps it was to do with being an inventor and always testing things out to see what happened, rather than just assuming what something (or someone) would be like.

'You shouldn't be prejudiced,' Sorrel said firmly to Burnet. 'Firstly, there aren't any goodies and baddies in the Wild World, as a very wise starling once said. And secondly, it's silly to dislike whole groups of creatures, because within a group all the individuals will be different – like we three are different from each other. I say we try to meet this rat and hear what it has to say.'

'But I've heard bad things about them,' said Burnet.

'Well, how about you reserve your judgement until you've actually got to know one, and then you can make up your own mind?'

At this, Burnet looked a little bit ashamed. 'Oh,

I know you're right, Sorrel. I think it's because I'm a bit frightened.'

'Don't worry,' said Cumulus reassuringly. 'I am, too. Things we don't know much about are often scary – and here we are, in a place we've never been before, in daylight, me almost invisible, when a creature we've never met before pops up and says—'

'ARE YOU THREE PIXIES COMING OR WOT?' squeaked the rat's voice again from the dark grating, making all three of them jump out of their skins.

'Now, listen up,' the high voice continued. 'I'm Barry – and if you're wonderin', yes, I 'eard your little discussion about my kind just now, and I'll be honest, it do 'urt. But, then again, I ain't surprised by it, for I've 'eard far worse said about rats. Mortals, in particular, call us all sorts of 'orrible names, for all we got in common with 'em. Or p'raps because of it, I sometimes think.'

Burnet flushed a deep red colour and bowed very low. 'I'm ever so sorry, Mr Barry, sir. My name is Burnet, and this is Cumulus and Sorrel. We are Hidden Folk – please don't let my ignorant comments colour what you think of our kind.'

'What, be prejudiced, you mean?' he replied, wryly. 'Course I won't. I was brought up better'n that, unlike some. Now, follow me, awwight?' And with a twitch of his whiskers, he dived back into the grating beneath the block of flats, and disappeared.

There was nothing for it but to follow, and, with a last look up at the bright, early-morning sky, the three Hidden Folk crept beneath the building, Sorrel going first and grabbing on to Barry's velvety tail as the rat led them into the darkness, who knows where.

21

Be lucky

*Cumulus, Burnet and Sorrel venture deep inside
a Mortal home, and what they find there
changes everything – and everyone.*

I n most buildings there's what we humans think
of as the rooms, and then a whole network of
other spaces that we know nothing about. At home
there's the kitchen, the bathroom, some bedrooms
and the lounge or front room or sitting room or
living room – whatever you like to call it. And there
may be other rooms, like a loo or a study or a games
room or den. At school there are the classrooms and
corridors, the offices, the staff room, the toilets, the
labs, the assembly hall and all the rest of it. But
between and around and under and over these
rooms run ventilation ducts, channels for water
pipes or disused chimneys, underfloor gaps or crawl
spaces, vents, grilles and gratings, and lots of interesting cracks and crevices besides. Our view of a
building is only one way of looking at it, and we

often share our warm and cosy habitat without knowing it. And given that we've built our homes in places where animals used to live, quite rightly so, too.

It was the first time the three Hidden Folk had ever been inside a building, so the network of spaces was all very new to them. They didn't get even a glimpse of the flats or stairwells the Mortals occupied; those parts weren't important to them, and were best avoided. Instead, Barry led them through a maze of dark corridors and passageways, some relatively clean, some full of dust. Sometimes, as they passed close to a kitchen in one of the flats, they could smell what the Mortals who lived there were having for breakfast; at one point they nearly choked on a sickeningly artificial aroma of flowers as they passed the air vent for a bathroom where someone had recently sprayed air freshener.

'Could be *a lot* worse, believe me,' said Barry, grimly. 'Sometimes you 'ave to hold yer breath going past that one.'

Sorrel found it all completely fascinating, and kept falling behind to look at how the pipes and ducts and joists were made.

At last they came to a brick chamber where a little light filtered in from somewhere above, and it was here that Barry stopped and turned to face them. 'This is as far as I go, mateys,' he said. 'Yer on yer own from 'ere, awwight?'

'What do you mean?' asked Cumulus. 'Is it dangerous?'

'Look,' the rat replied, 'I'm a kind-hearted soul, Pan knows. I like to help a fellow creature out, if I can, and the moment I seen you lot out on the grass there – well, I knew what I 'ad to do. But us residents all have our own areas, see? It's how we get by in 'ere. It's not like the outdoors, where each creature can 'ave a big territory. Sure, we all share some of the through routes, and fourteen and an 'alf emergency exits, but beyond that we keep to ourselves – not least 'cos us rats are far cleaner than *some* I could mention . . .' Here he coughed, and the cough somehow contained the word 'mice'.

The three of them must have looked worried, for Barry's clever little face softened, and he set his whiskers at a friendly angle. 'You'll be all right,' he said. 'I promise. Just carry on through that gap, shin up the pipe you'll find in there – on the outside of it, that is, don't try and get in it – and then, Bob's yer uncle.'

'Or aunt,' said Sorrel.

'And w-what will we find there?' asked Burnet,

in a slightly wavering voice.

'That is for you lot to discover, because, truth be told, I'm not sure of the ins and outs of it meself. Now, I'm going to head back out and let your starling friend know where you are. Stay safe and be lucky, awwight?'

One by one they all shook the rat's little pink paw, Cumulus needing two goes at it because Barry couldn't see what he was supposed to take hold of.

'I hope we'll meet again,' said Burnet.

'Not if I see you first, pal,' grinned the rat, and disappeared.

After climbing up the pipe, the three Hidden Folk found themselves on a dirty ledge, with no idea at all of why Barry the rat had told them to get up there. What on earth, they all wondered, had he expected them to find? Looking around, they could see no immediate danger, but they were all feeling a bit nervous, and spoke to one another only in the quietest of whispers. At least it was dark, so they couldn't see each other as clearly as in daylight, something that made Cumulus feel a bit better about things.

Sorrel found an old metal screw discarded amid the brick dust and held it up triumphantly to show the others.

'Put it in your backpack!' hissed Burnet, giving a thumbs-up.

And then, they all froze.

Two voices were approaching from somewhere, quite loud and careless. It wasn't Mortal speech, and nor was it the Rodent Argot shared by mice and rats.

'And so I said, "Look, you're quite safe here, and there's nothing we can do for now," but it didn't make any difference.'

'So *then* what did you say?' came the reply. The conversation began to fade into the distance again. 'Well, then I said . . .' the first voice replied.

The three Hidden Folk looked at one another in the dimness, eyes wide. The voices sounded both familiar and unfamiliar, which made them feel anxious and curious at the same time.

'We need to work out how to get a look at whoever that was,' Sorrel whispered at last.

It didn't take long. Barry had directed them to the ledge because, if you climbed on to a piece of two-by-four, you could see over a joist into the chamber beyond. And it was an extraordinary sight.

Light filtered down through a long gap in what must have been some floorboards, which here formed the ceiling of a small, rectangular chamber.

Its floor was perfectly clean, and the whole space was warmed by another copper pipe in one corner, which carried hot water behind the walls and into a radiator in one of the Mortals' rooms. The chamber's walls were lined with ingeniously fashioned cupboards and shelves made not from wood but from colourful cards and what looked like empty raisin boxes. Near the copper pipe were two comfy-looking beanbags made from Mortals' lost socks that had been carefully cut down, stitched into spheres, and stuffed with lentils.

Just then, two little people walked into the room, one short and round, the other about as tall as Cumulus. They wore colourful outfits of Mortal-made cloth, which made them look strange (though Sorrel, in a frogskin onesie, was hardly one to judge). But as oddly dressed as they were, it was immediately clear that they were some kind of Hidden Folk.

The trio immediately ducked back down behind the joist and stared at one another with their mouths open.

'Are they . . . ?' mouthed Burnet, pointing in the general direction of the two figures.

'I think so! I can't believe it!' hissed Sorrel.

Cumulus, being both taller and almost invisible, cautiously peeked back into the room.

'Well, look, we can only do our best,' the tall one was saying. 'I'm sure it'll all work out for the best in the end.'

'I hope so,' said the shorter one. 'You know how I worry.'

'I do, dear one. You are the kindest of Hobs.'

'What's a Hob?' hissed Sorrel and Burnet together – but Cumulus flapped an empty sleeve at them, for quiet.

'Anyway, my love, what shall we have for dinner?' the voice continued. 'I quite fancy the rest of that crisp, you know, and perhaps that long spaghetti strand we found.'

'What's spaghetti?' whispered Burnet, at which Cumulus turned to the others, pulled a cross face and went '*Shhhhh!*' very loudly.

'What was that?' said the first voice.

'I heard it too,' whispered the second voice. 'It came from behind the wall. Do you think it was a cockroach?'

'No, it didn't sound like one.'

'One of the mouse clan, perhaps? There are rather a lot of them this year.'

The voices were getting louder and closer to where Cumulus, Sorrel and Burnet crouched.

'Oh, for the love of Pan,' said Cumulus suddenly,

standing up again. 'I don't even know why we're hiding. Get up, you two.' So, a little shamefacedly, they did.

The five little beings, craning to peer over the top of the joist, regarded one another cautiously.

'We apologize for intruding on your home like this – I know it must seem rude. I'm Cumulus, and these are my friends Burnet and Sorrel. I'm sorry about being invisible; it's a recent development. There's really no cause for alarm.'

Strangely, however, the duo were neither fazed by Cumulus's appearance (or lack of it) nor surprised to meet more of their own kind – although they didn't seem pleased to find intruders in their home.

'Why are you here, and what do you want?' asked the shorter of the pair, stepping forward to confront them.

'We – er, we were told to come here by Barry the rat,' said Cumulus. 'May I ask – you described yourselves as "Hobs" just now—'

'What else would we be?'

'It's just that . . . Well, we're Hidden Folk, and—'

'Why did Barry send you here? What do you want?'

'I don't suppose we could come in and explain, could we?'

'Absolutely not,' said the figure. 'You could be anyone – you could be dangerous fugitives, for all we know! And, in any case, creeping around the emergency exits and spying on people – well, it's not polite.'

'I know, and we really are very sorry,' replied Cumulus – but just then everyone stopped talking because Burnet, face scrunched up with misery, had silently begun to cry. Grief for their friend, two sleepless nights, the excitement and fear of their search, and then a telling-off from strangers had proved too much.

'Oh, no, please don't cry!' cried Sorrel.

'Dear Burnet, what's wrong?' asked Cumulus, and they both hugged and tried to comfort their friend. But Burnet just sobbed and sobbed.

'I'm – just – so – *tired* . . . and I – I – miss Moss so – very, *very* – much. And my – my knees are disappearing, and I thought – I thought we'd all be – be – together again by now – and – we're *not*!'

At that, all three of them began to weep, and they hugged one another and let all their sadness come tumbling out. Sometimes, that's the best thing to do. It might not fix the problem you're having, but if you squash down or store up your sad or cross feelings they'll only cause havoc later by making you accidentally misbehave.

'Oh dear, oh dear, this is ever so upsetting. Please, please, do come in after all,' came a tentative voice from the other side of the joist. 'We're very sorry not to have been more welcoming. It's just – well, we had our reasons. Oh, now I understand, I feel *terrible* . . .'

So, after drying their eyes and blowing their noses, the trio clambered up and over the wooden joist and into the cosy little room.

'I'm Macadam,' said the shorter of the couple, bowing low, 'and this is Minaret. We're Hobs. And through there, in the other room, you'll find your friend Moss.'

22

The party

Robin's Lore.

What a reunion it was! Cumulus, Burnet and Sorrel rushed in to find Moss propped up in a little wooden bed, looking very pale but grinning from ear to ear. Minaret and Macadam brought stools for everyone to sit on, and then went to prepare some food and drink for their guests, leaving the four friends to kiss and hug one another, exclaim over their adventures, and fill one another in on the events of the last few days.

Moss was terribly concerned about Burnet's increasing invisibility, but Burnet promised that it didn't hurt in the least bit and smiled extra-bravely. Cumulus probably smiled as well, but none of them could see.

'I don't remember much about it, fortunately,' said Moss, when Sorrel asked what had happened.

'I'm told a cat got me, but all I can remember is waking up here, in bed. Apparently it brought me in its mouth and dropped me on the floor of one of the Mortals' areas – a food-making room, I think it was. Min was scavenging for scraps and heard a commotion, peeked from under a cabinet and saw me, then ran out and dragged me to safety while Mac made a loud noise to distract the cat. Wasn't that brave?'

'Gosh, it really was!' replied Sorrel, impressed. 'And how are you feeling now?'

'Oh, much better than at first – especially now that you're all here. I'm afraid I haven't been the easiest patient to look after – I knew you'd all be worried sick, you see, so I've found it hard to just lie here and rest.'

'Well, we're here now – and we're all together again!' said Burnet, taking one of Moss's hands which lay on the patterned blanket, and giving it a loving squeeze.

'And those two are Hobs,' said Cumulus, musingly. 'Well, I never!'

'Oh, yes – what *are* Hobs?' asked Sorrel.

It was at that moment that Macadam and Minaret came back in, each carrying a tray piled high with food.

'Well,' said Minaret, setting a tray down at the foot of the bed and handing round a stack of plates made from beer-bottle lids. 'The long and the short of it is . . . we're Hidden Folk too! Just a slightly different kind.'

It was quite true. Wise old Cumulus had known it from the moment they saw them, for Hobs are simply another kind of Hidden Folk who prefer to live indoors. Mortals generally call them borrowers or hobgoblins, or *bwbach* in Wales and *bauchan* in Scotland. They have been in the Wild World for almost as long as Mortals have lived indoors, but Cumulus, Moss, Burnet and Sorrel had never met any of them before.

'So there *are* more of us still in the Wild World!' said Moss. 'Isn't that the best bit of news? Honestly, it was almost worth me being caught by a cat to find that out. Just think: we could have searched the outdoors part of the Mortals' Hive and never come across Min and Mac here at all.'

'And there are quite a lot of us in the Hive, you know,' said Macadam, dishing out fragments of Pom-Bears, cold spaghetti cut into sections and a Cocoa Puff each. 'In fact, a good few buildings around here are home to one or two of us. Not all, mind: some of the newer ones don't have enough gaps and crevices for us to live in, and some are too cold or too empty – or just not very nice.'

'So that's where the rest of our kind are now,' mused Cumulus, 'living indoors, in Mortals' Hives, instead of in the countryside!'

Minaret smiled. 'Some of us, yes. We decided to adapt, you see. The countryside was changing fast, with fewer safe places for us to live and be happy, and all the while the Hives were growing bigger and eating up more of the land. And Hidden Folk are a bit like pigeons and rats and squirrels: we're adaptable and resourceful, aren't we? We can live alongside Mortals, if we must – though lots of wild creatures can't.'

'Yes, we're lucky,' said Macadam. 'Though you know, there's more wildness here than you might expect – especially in the scruffier bits, where the Mortals don't try to make everything too neat. It can be ever so beautiful here in the Hive, if you know where to look.'

'Would you like to meet some more of us, now you're here?' asked Minaret. 'It's just us two in this particular building, but we could invite our friends over to meet you all. There's someone we particularly think Cumulus and Burnet should meet.'

'Oh, yes, a party!' cried Burnet, immediately

excited by the thought of cake and sweets and games. 'Let's do that!'

'Hmm, perhaps . . .' replied Cumulus, a little doubtfully. 'Is Moss well enough for that kind of excitement, do you think?'

'That's a good point. Are you very badly injured, Moss?' asked Sorrel.

'The good thing is that it doesn't hurt much any more,' said Moss, not quite answering the question.

'There's quite a lot of swelling where the cat's teeth went in, around Moss's back and tummy,' explained Macadam. 'It was quite infected at first, but Minaret here has been keeping it clean, haven't you, dearest? We're hoping it'll get better, Pan willing, given time.'

The party was planned for that night. Burnet had wanted to have it in the park, and Cumulus and Sorrel agreed that it would be nice to be out in the sunshine, where Spangle, Chip and Bud, and the four heroic pigeons could all join in the fun. But Mac and Min pointed out that Hobs were happier indoors, and, faced with a trip into the open air, many wouldn't come; not to mention the fact that

Moss was, for now, confined to bed. So it was agreed that Burnet would plan a party for their outdoor friends another time, and word was sent out to all the Hobs in the neighbouring tower blocks, flats and houses via a network of messengers, including house mice and rats – though, truth be told, the mice didn't make the best envoys, sometimes forgetting what they were supposed to say altogether, or getting the details all muddled up.

The new friends spent the afternoon getting to know one another, telling stories of distant cousins and ancestors, swapping recipes and ways to do things, and learning about each other's daily lives, while Moss lay in bed, resting and recovering, and sometimes joining in with the talk.

But there were moments when Moss was quiet, and just lay still and thought. Burnet had given back the acorn-cup hat, and with it had come flashes of memory about the cat attack – of being carried, dangling, through the streets – and with the memories came a horrible leftover fear, as though it were all happening again.

While Mac and Min did some cooking for the party, and Sorrel and Burnet went off to explore the block of flats, Cumulus came to sit on Moss's bed. The two of them held hands and didn't say much;

they just enjoyed being together again.

'What are you thinking about?' asked Cumulus, after a while.

'Mostly about how stupid I was – that it was all my fault.'

'The cat, you mean?'

'Yes.'

'Oh, Moss. It could have happened to any of us.'

'No, it's because I was greedy – I wanted more Mortal food, and I didn't think. I didn't even tell anyone where I was going. And by making you search for me, I put everyone in danger. I'm so sorry, Cumulus . . .' and a tear slid down Moss's face.

'Oh, Moss, this isn't like you. You know that everyone makes mistakes, don't you? The important thing is what you learn from them, and whether you can make them count.'

At last there came a knock at the door, and Mac and Min rushed to show the guests in. How interesting they all looked in their streetwise Hive fashions – one was dressed entirely in sweet wrappers! And all were excited to meet more of their kind.

In the main chamber two tables were loaded with food, and many of the guests had bought dishes of their own, too: a morsel of tuna stolen from a cat's bowl; a beetroot carved with a happy face like a tiny pumpkin; pink icing from a child's birthday cake, rolled into balls; some odd pellety things that looked as though they'd been stolen from a hamster's cage, which nobody ate; and some delicious parsnip and leek soup garnished with the tiniest florets of cauliflower imaginable (the Hob who brought it was a vegan called Lintel). Instead of cowslip cordial they drank blackberry juice, for blackberries grow on brambles, and brambles can be found almost anywhere, including lots of parks in nearly every single Mortal Hive.

Everyone milled around, chatting and eating and introducing themselves to one another, while Minaret and Macadam, as hosts, talked in turn to everyone and made sure they all had enough to eat and drink. Burnet began a very interesting conversation about the weather and the seasons with a Hob called Verdigris, while Sorrel chatted to two friends called Corbel and Bitumen, who knew a lot about the history of all kinds of Hidden Folk and how they came to live in all the places they inhabited now.

Cumulus was looking at Burnet and wondering why nobody had remarked on their invisible body parts when there came a voice from close by.

'Hello, you must be Cumulus. I'm Feldspar.'

Cumulus whipped around but there was nobody there, only a pair of callused feet and above them a pink ball of icing, floating in mid-air.

'Don't be alarmed or embarrassed,' came the voice again. 'I'm quite real – I'm what we call a "Fader". Mac and Min thought we should meet.'

'I'm sorry to seem rude – I was just taken by surprise. So this is . . . it's happening to Hobs, too?'

'Oh, yes, of course – for quite some time now.'

'And are you . . . are you completely *bare-naked*?' Cumulus asked, looking Feldspar up and down.

'I am, yes. Why not?'

'Gosh, well, I suppose so,' replied Cumulus. 'And have you got used to being invisible? Will it come to feel all right?'

'In some ways, although I'd much rather it wasn't happening, wouldn't you? I'm not ready to leave the Wild World just yet.'

'Leave the Wild World? Whatever do you mean?' asked Cumulus.

'Well – yes,' replied Feldspar. 'Do you mean to tell me you don't know what's happening to you?

You've never heard of Robin's Lore?'

'Of course I've heard of Robin Goodfellow – the oldest of all us Hidden Folk. And the legends say that Robin actually met Pan once, but that's all I know. But what is Robin's Lore?'

'Robin was the first of the Hidden Folk to move indoors, and after living in all sorts of Mortal settlements, ended up here, in the Hive. We were friends – well, as much as anyone could be with such a mischievous, unpredictable type! But Robin was wise, too – which you would be, if you'd lived in the Wild World since its very dawn.

'Anyway, Robin left behind three truths we call the Lore. The first was that Hidden Folk can only be killed by Mortalkind or by Mortal-made things, which I'm sure you already know. The second was that Mortals will one day be our friends, and because of that, we should try to look after them. And the third was that our kind will fade quietly out of the Wild World when our work here is done.'

Cumulus's head was reeling. 'Wait – so you're telling me I'm . . . *dying?*'

'Oh, no, no, no – absolutely not! The Lore says we just pass into the next place, wherever that might be. Robin never seemed to mind about it, so we try not to worry too much, either. I'm sorry, Cumulus –

I didn't realize you didn't know all this. It must come as a bit of a shock.'

'It does. But what do you mean about Robin leaving this Lore behind?'

'Well, the fading seems to start with the oldest, you see,' said Feldspar. 'And, being so incredibly ancient . . . well, Robin Goodfellow's been gone from the Wild World for a long time now.'

Moss was sitting up in bed and chatting to a Hob called Dormer, who had cool spiky hair. Dormer was one of those funny, warm people you instantly like, even if you're not really feeling up to a party, or you find meeting new people a bit overwhelming. They were about the same age, and quickly found themselves discussing everything from their favourite foods (honey cake for Moss) to their respective outfits ('Nice hat!' said Dormer), and everything that had happened in their lives so far. It's so nice when you meet someone like that.

'So what's next, once you're back up and about?' Dormer asked. 'Will you make a home in the Hive now, or journey back to Ash Row – or perhaps you'll all go and stay by the Folly Brook again?'

'We haven't really talked about that yet,' said Moss. 'I do want to find a new home one day, but—'

Just then, Cumulus banged on the copper pipe with a matchstick, a signal for everyone to hush, because a speech was about to be made. Fourteen little faces turned expectantly to look.

'Ahem,' Cumulus began.

'Boo!' shouted Burnet, overexcitedly.

'Shhh!' hissed everyone else.

'Good evening, everyone, and thank you for coming. It's been very good to meet you, and to discover that we are not the last of our kind after all.'

'Hear, hear!' cried Macadam, while Minaret did one of those loud whistles some people can do by sticking their fingers in their mouth.

'As you can see, I've almost completely faded, and my friend Burnet here is disappearing from the ground up. Now, I realize that you're all familiar with this condition, given that Feldspar here – wait, over there – Feldspar's only a pair of feet now, and I'm told other Hobs have disappeared completely, never to be seen again. But for us four, all this has been very new, and very frightening, and we didn't have a clue what it meant.

'But now, Feldspar has told me about Robin's

Lore, and how it states that our kind will fade quietly from the Wild World when our work here is done. Well, you might be all right with that, but I'm not. The four of us have seen a great many things on our way to the Hive, and it's obvious that Mortals aren't ready to look after the Wild World yet – not properly. There's still a lot of work to do, as far as I'm concerned!'

Alarmed by Feldspar's talk of 'the next place', and relieved to have come up with a plan, Cumulus was talking fast and excitedly. It was hard not to get swept up in the speech.

'It's time we found ourselves a new role – not as guardians or caretakers, but as teachers – teachers of Mortalkind. I haven't worked out all the details, but we know of a child who can speak the Wild Argot. I propose that we find her, and ask for her help. We'll start small, by showing her how to make things better for our old friends, the Garden People, back at Ash Row. Then, if the fading starts to get better, we'll know it's what Pan wants us to do. And then we'll work out how to scale it up and just . . . save the whole world, and the Hidden Folk at the same time!'

There was a wild burst of applause. As the uproar subsided, Burnet and Sorrel, who had been listening open-mouthed, rushed over and they all sat around Moss's bed so they could talk.

'Is it true?' asked Moss, reaching out for Cumulus's invisible hand and gazing at where their old friend's face must be.

'I think it is,' replied Cumulus. 'It means our kind are fading from the Wild World, starting with the oldest among us – so after me and Burnet, Sorrel will be next. You've got lots of time left, though, Moss, don't you worry.' And Moss felt a comforting pat on the arm.

Sorrel looked thoughtful. 'Do you really believe in Robin's Lore, then, Cumulus?'

'Well – yes,' replied Cumulus. 'Why, don't you?'

'It's an interesting story, I suppose, but is it reason enough to take such a big decision? To actually contact Mortals, on purpose? I suppose what I'm saying is – are you *sure*?'

Burnet chipped in. 'Look, Sorrel. You once said that nobody can be sure that Pan exists, and this is the same thing. Whether Robin's Lore is true or just a Hob legend, trying to make life better for other creatures can only ever be a good thing. And, in any case, there's one thing Cumulus is definitely right about. We can't do nothing. We have to *try*.'

'That's true. It's just . . . I'm not sure saving the world is as easy as all that, I suppose.'

While the others talked, Moss's eyes had filled with tears. 'I don't want you to fade away and disappear – any of you! I want us to stay together in the Wild World, for ever, just like we always said we would!'

'And we will,' said Cumulus, whose voice was determined. 'That's *exactly* what's going to happen – just you wait and see.'

For the rest of the party, everyone mingled and talked earnestly to one another about what Cumulus had said about being useful.

'What's all this "we", anyway?' asked the Hob dressed in sweet wrappers. 'For one thing, they're Hidden Folk and we're Hobs – there's no "we" about it. And for another, I'm pretty sure *I'm* useful already. I'm a walking work of art!'

'I think it's good for them to go on their quest if they want to,' said another. 'But do you *really* think Mortals are likely to change their ways?'

However, Dormer, the spiky-haired Hob, went around telling everyone that it was a brilliant idea, and that they'd all feel more satisfied with life if they had an important role, as Hidden Folk had in days gone by.

As for Min and Mac, they weren't quite sure they believed in Pan, or in Robin Goodfellow's teachings, but if there was a way to stay together for ever – even if it was an outside chance – they wanted to take it. Whether in the Hive or the countryside, the Wild World was a beautiful place, and they didn't want to leave it yet.

Moss sat up in bed watching the party and thinking about Cumulus's speech. The idea of teaching Mortals to be guardians felt far too big a task for someone so small – someone who, in their heart of hearts, would have just liked to go home and live quietly back at dear old Ash Row.

'I think the party will be over soon,' came Cumulus's voice from close by. 'We've got an awful lot to talk about later, and some very big decisions to make. But before all that, why don't you recite this year's ballad, before everyone goes home?'

Moss's heart thumped with sudden nerves. '*Now?* To all these strangers?'

'You don't have to, if it's not ready,' said Cumulus kindly.

When they'd arrived at the Folly, it had felt good

to be the one to tell Sorrel their adventures, to choose the right words so that everyone listened and smiled. After all, they could all rustle up a bit of lunch, but none of them could tell a story anything like as well as Moss could. And what had Roger the pigeon said about bravery? He'd said it wasn't about being fearless, but doing the thing you're scared of anyway.

'I want to do it,' Moss said, with a smile.

So Cumulus banged on the pipe again with the matchstick, and everyone fell quiet.

'Cumulus suggested I recite my twenty-one-verse annual ballad,' Moss began, a little hesitantly. 'But I can't. It's – it's not right.'

There was a silence. Macadam and Minaret, who were holding hands, looked at one another, hoping Moss was all right.

'I wanted the ballad to be a record of all our adventures. And it was really exciting – you know, like the old legends and stories of our kind. But I didn't include everything that happened to us, or tell the truth about how it all felt. For instance, I didn't write a verse about how I was caught by a cat, because I was ashamed of it, and I was worried it would spoil the whole thing.

'But Cumulus got me thinking, and I've decided

that this ballad should include the times when we were frightened, or got lost, or were cross with one another. And perhaps if I tell it properly, it could help warn others about cats, too – and then a good thing might come out of my mistake.'

As the gathering broke out in applause, Moss looked around at all the warm, kindly faces, some known and loved, but many entirely new. Several people were nodding and smiling, and nobody was saying how silly it was to have made a mistake. In fact, Sorrel and Burnet were cheering, and though it was hard to tell, Cumulus seemed to be wiping away a proud tear.

'Thank you in advance for listening,' said Moss, smiling back at everyone. 'My ballad now has *twenty-two* verses, so here goes . . .

It was the kind of March day that feels springish,
Though the weather had not yet warmed up
When we set out to walk to the Folly
And meet Sorrel, and Eddy, and Cluck . . .'

A Note From the Author

This is a story about the secret world of wild creatures that exists all around us at every moment, something which most grown-ups (and many children) have no idea exists.

If you're a noticing kind of person, as I am, you might well pick up clues to this secret world when you're playing outside: things like neatly nibbled nutshells, interesting-looking holes and paths, mysterious droppings, or footprints in mud or snow. From these clues you can work out who you share your garden, street, playground or park with, what they've been up to, and what life is like for your smaller neighbours, whether they're feathered or furred, moist-skinned or prickly, have an armoured exoskeleton or wear an acorn-cup hat. You might even have the very great honour of giving them a helping hand one day.

But if, despite your noticingness, you find it hard to believe in Hidden Folk – perhaps because you've never seen one, and neither have any of your friends – that's completely all right. Even the brief glimpse I had was accidental, because over the course of many centuries they have perfected the art of not being observed by us. And as well as that, you might have come across some ridiculous cartoons or silly stories about magical elves and goblins, comical gnomes or flying fairies with sparkly wings, which have made you feel sure that such preposterous creatures don't exist.

And you'd be right. Hidden Folk aren't magic, and they don't have sparkly wings. They live by hunting, fishing and gathering wild foods, just as wild animals do. They have been in the Wild World since for ever, which is a lot longer than us humans, and once lived in all the different parts of these islands and in many other countries, too – although there are far fewer of them now than once upon a time.

When there were more of them and fewer of us, they were seen a little more often, and we humans gave them names, just as we named the birds and plants and insects and everything else: we called them hidden folk and little grey men, elves and fairies, goblins and gnomes, imps, sprites and, in the West Country, pixies (or piskies). The Romans referred to them as *Genii locorum*, which means 'the guardians of a place'; they were known as sidhe in Ireland, brownies in Scotland, huldufólk in Iceland and by lots of other names across Europe and beyond. But the truth is that whatever we choose to call them isn't what they call themselves.

One more thing. I'm sure it comes as no surprise to you to learn that all the birds and insects and animals and Hidden Folk can talk to one another, more or less, using what's called the 'Wild Argot': a basic language that all of nature shares. Each species speaks it slightly differently, but they can all make themselves understood by one another, and in fact the only creature that's forgotten how to communicate with the Wild World is we humans. But I suspect that, in fact, most of us have just stopped listening – which perhaps comes to the same thing.

Melissa Harrison, spring 2021

Acknowledgements

Firstly, thank you to Barry, Rachel and everyone else at Chicken House for seeing promise in my early draft, and helping to turn it into the book it needed to become.

Thank you, always, to my agent Jenny Hewson, who knows what's what.

Thank you to early readers Peter Rogers, Paraic O'Donnell and Saskia Daniel; to Josie George and Isabel Chua for help with names; and to Sarah Fisher, Nicola Guereca and Nick Redman for lending me calm, quiet places to write, when I really needed them.

I'm so grateful to the Trustees of the Estate of the late Denys Watkins-Pitchford for their kind permission to make reference to characters and locations from B.B.'s classic *The Little Grey Men* books – both of which I highly recommend.

Extract from the *The Wild Lone: The Story of a Pytchley Fox*, B.B. (Eyre & Spottiswoode, 1938) reprinted by permission of David Higham Associates.

Watching the Wild World

MARCH

Listen out for the first blackbird song of the year. Your local blackbird may have several singing spots, high up where his voice can carry. He'll continue singing until the end of July, to tell any rivals where his breeding territory is. If you listen carefully, you'll hear that his song will have a twizzle or flourish that's unique to him.

APRIL

Do any of the ponds or ditches near you have spawn in them? Can you work out who it belongs to? Frogspawn is laid in clumps, toad spawn in chains, and newt spawn as individual eggs, stuck to leaves. Be sure to leave it where it is, but if you keep going back you'll see the tadpoles hatch this month – and see what arrives to eat them, too.

MAY

Find out what time the sun rises, and persuade a grown-up to get up at least half an hour earlier. Go somewhere with lots of trees and bushes (and therefore lots of birds), where you can hear the dawn chorus. It's at its loudest and most magnificent this month, and very few Mortals hear it, as we're known to be a very lazy species indeed . . .

JUNE

Can you spot any swifts, swallows or house martins hunting for flying insects high overhead? See if you can track these summer visitors to the buildings where they nest, usually just beneath the roof. Swallows and house martins make cups from mud, while swifts nest in crevices. The more insects there are, the more of these magical birds.

JULY

How many secret paths made by wild creatures can you find? Look out for the gaps deer, badgers and foxes use to pass through hedges (and, sometimes, the hairs they leave there, caught on twigs). In long grass, you might find the trails rabbits, hedgehogs, stoats and weasels make. Look out (and listen out) for grasshoppers this month, too!

AUGUST

How many kinds of butterflies and moths live near you, and what are they up to this month? Which flowers do they sip nectar from, and which do they ignore? If you look up the species of plant their caterpillars eat, you might find the tiny eggs the adults lay, often on the underside of the leaves – or you might find their caterpillars nibbling away. The more plants there are whose flowers provide nectar for butterflies and moths to drink, or whose leaves can be eaten by their caterpillars, the more there'll be next year.

More to Discover

Things to read:
The Little Grey Men by B.B.
*The Little Grey Men Go Down the
    Bright Stream* by B.B.
Animal Tracks and Signs by Preben Bang and Preben
    Dahlstrom
RSPB The Nature Tracker's Handbook by Nick Baker
Wonderland: A Year of Britain's Wildlife, Day by Day by
    Brett Westwood and Stephen Moss
How to Help a Hedgehog and Protect a Polar Bear by
    Jess French and Angela Keoghan

Things to watch:
Springwatch and *Autumnwatch* (BBC Two, ongoing)
Oak Tree: Nature's Greatest Survivor (available on
    YouTube)
Directed by Stephen de Vere:
    *Through the Garden Gate: A Diary of the English
        Countryside*
    Summer in the Meadow: Diary of a Vanishing World
    Return to the River: Diary of a Wildlife Cameraman
    (available on DVD from bit.ly/stephendevere)

Things to do:

Take part in the Big Butterfly Count, July–August:
bit.ly/baoat_butterfly

Join in with events at your local Wildlife Trust:
bit.ly/baoat_wildlife

Learn natural navigation:
bit.ly/baoat_ navigation

Build a rubber-band car:
bit.ly/baoat_car